The Man Who Walked Backwards
AND OTHER STORIES

S. Ramakrishnan is an influential writer of modern Tamil literature. A prolific author, his oeuvre includes ten novels, twenty collections of short stories, sixty collections of articles, twenty books for children, three books of translation and nine plays. Among the many awards he has received are the Sahitya Akademi Award in 2018, the Tagore Literary Award for his novel *Yamam*, Iyal Award, Maxim Gorky Award and Periyar Award. His writings have been translated and published in English, Malayalam, Hindi, Bengali, Telugu, Kannada and French. He lives in Chennai with his wife Chandra Prabha and sons Hariprasad and Akash.

Prabha Sridevan was Judge of the Madras High Court (2000–2010) and Chairperson of the Intellectual Property Appellate Board (2011–2013). She has judged crucial cases related to freedom of speech, gender equality, housework and women's labour, and patenting and licensing of pharmaceutical drugs. As a translator, her published works include *Seeing in the Dark* (2015), *Echoes of the Veena and Other Stories* (2019) which won the Valley of Words Translation Award, *Meeran's Stories* (2021), *Essays of U Ve Sa* (co-translated with Pradeep Chakravarthy) (2022), *R. Chudamani* (Makers of Indian Literature Series) and *If There Is a God and Other Stories* (2022).

The Man Who Walked Backwards

AND OTHER STORIES

S. RAMAKRISHNAN

Translated from the original Tamil by

PRABHA SRIDEVAN

Orient BlackSwan

THE MAN WHO WALKED BACKWARDS AND OTHER STORIES

ORIENT BLACKSWAN PRIVATE LIMITED

Registered Office
3-6-752 Himayatnagar, Hyderabad 500 029, Telangana, India
e-mail: centraloffice@orientblackswan.com

Other Offices
Bengaluru, Chennai, Guwahati, Hyderabad, Kolkata,
Mumbai, New Delhi, Noida, Patna, Visakhapatnam

First published by Orient Blackswan Private Limited 2023

ISBN 978-93-5442-437-3

Typeset in
Garamond Premier Pro 11.5/14.5
by Le Studio Graphique, Gurgaon 122 007

038048

Printed in India at
Thomson Press, New Delhi 110 020

Published by
Orient Blackswan Private Limited
3-6-752 Himayatnagar, Hyderabad 500 029, Telangana, India
e-mail: info@orientblackswan.com

Contents

Author's Note

There is a Mulla story where he searches for his keys in the road. "Why do you search for your key here? You misplaced it at home, didn't you?" his friend asks him. Mulla replies that it is bright only out in the road; if you search where there is light, even if you don't find your house-keys, you may find something else. Our lives exist between the space where we have lost something and the space where we search for it.

But writers are not like Mulla; they do not search where there is light, they search in the dark. They do not know what they have lost. Because it is not something that *they* lost, it is what their ancestors had lost, what the culture had lost, or their family, or something that was wrenched away from them by force. People search for the many things they have lost in many ways.

Some animals can see clearly in the dark. They know that darkness is merely diminished light. Writers too search for the things and the people they have lost within the darkness of memory. At the age of thirty, they seek solutions for the hurt they suffered in childhood.

I am searching in the dark too, through my stories. This is not a dark that is familiar, it is a dark created over ages, by wilful acts of human beings. Don't we close the windows during the day to create an atmosphere of darkness? The act of my writing is a search in the darkness created by humankind, a darkness that inflicts suffering.

Till I was five, I thought that the sun rose only in my village, and that the moon lit up only the sky I could see. It was difficult to accept the truth that it is the same sun, sky and earth that is shared by the whole world. With the realisation of this irrefutable truth, far-off cities, countries and people became very close, as near as the other side of the coin.

But in truth, there are two suns and two moons: a sun out there and the other in my heart. The one in my heart never disappears. I was born in the *karisal* region, the land of the black soil, where the sun was always strong. It continues to glow in my heart, and its light is revealed in my stories too. When we were young boys, we would discuss if the world was small or large. As I grew older, I learnt whose world was narrow and whose was wide. The world is indeed very small for business people who travel thousands of miles in one day. For a bed-ridden invalid, one day stretches for ever. While for us adults, the world is very big, for children, it is just a plaything like a football.

For a woman born in my village, who gets married there and dies there, the expanse of the world hardly matters. The world to her is not a physical space, it is an internal space. This world as we know it does not remember persons like her. So as a creator, I want to understand her and people like her in whose hearts lies a universal love fashioning a sea, a mountain, a waterfall, and a forest—all within themselves. It is them that I write about.

When my grandmother wanted a photograph of herself, her family did not permit her. During a temple festival, she went to a studio and took a photo. She did not know where to hide the picture. She kept it amidst her sarees. It was found out and her family made her throw it in the fire with her own hands. In silence, she watched her image burn. In my stories, I write about the sound of that fire and that wordless silence.

The people in my stories do not face big challenges, they do not seek big victories. They are the dice that Time plays with. They face humiliation and rejection within their family. But they also find their own redemption from this suffering. The mother in

"Amma's Last Swim" conquers her rage by swimming, a path that she discovered for herself.

In my stories, I mostly speak of people who have been ignored, humiliated, persecuted or insulted. The world does not understand them. No one pays heed to their voices that weep silently. As a creator, I take their side. I share their sorrows with the world. I argue their case before my readers.

Prabha Sridevan has selected the best of my short stories and has translated them very well. For her selection and the care with which she has done her translation, she deserves many thanks. I convey my deepest gratitude to the publisher Orient BlackSwan, to my wife Chandraprabha who loves me and my writing, and my sons Hari and Akash.

Translator's Note

The best thing that happened to me after my retirement was my discovery that I could translate. It obsesses me in a fantastic way. The diverse worlds I have occupied, the worlds of my authors, have given me a gift that is without a parallel. I once heard, or perhaps read, a translator saying that it is not necessary for a translator to enjoy the original text for translation. I do not agree with that, but each to their own taste. While I am translating, I wear the shoes of the author and live the stories that I work on. And I rather love the shoes.

S. Ramakrishnan's stories, like the pigeons in one of them, flew into my soul. I could not let go of the people in the stories: the mother who swam and swam, the father who recorded the rain, the estate owner who built a house for the wind and the rain, the thief at whose touch withered trees bloomed. Who are they? Did they evolve out of lives like ours? Do those women and men lie dormant in each one of us? The persons he writes about are people who are alone in an inexplicable way. Listen to Narasimhan of "Sitridazh": "All my poems were published exclusively in that small journal, a *sitridazh*, a zine. No big magazine ever came forward to ask me for a poem. How lovely is this word, 'sitridazh'! Sounds like a wild flower. But sitridazh is really like a small brook. There are some fishes that live only in brooks." The characters are all like that—fish in small brooks that really do not miss the ocean. These stories do not let you go even after you have read the last line, and in my case, even after I had written the last line.

I don't know who taught Amma to swim. But for as long as I could remember, for Amma bathing meant swimming. Even in the rainy season. She would not bathe at home.

Appa could not swim. He worked as the village postman.

We moved to Tekkudi because Appa was posted there and then at some point, we bought a house and settled down in the village. My sister was born in Tekkudi. Appa would only be transferred within the district, so we never had to move house. I studied in Tekkudi Primary School.

In the beginning, we used to live on the street by the Panchayat office. It was Amma who pushed for the purchase of an old house in the *agraharam*, the area where the Brahmins lived. In the past, that agraharam had been very wealthy. Gradually, the inhabitants deserted the area and only one or two houses remained occupied. Two houses had totally broken down, and there were plants growing through the crevices of the dilapidated walls. Since the owners had gone away to America, no one bothered to repair them.

Even the house we bought was from someone who was settled in London. We got it for a very low price. The house was a large one, with six rooms. There was a big terrace, a well, and plantain trees in the backyard. We were a family of just four. So Appa had asked if we really needed such a big house for just the four of us.

"Let us have a large house at least," Amma had said.

It was an expression of her anger, and Appa knew that. Amma had the house painted dark blue. No one else in the village had a house that colour. So that was the unique feature by which our house came to be identified.

Amma never spoke much. She was always lost in thought and liked a quiet house. She frowned even if a crow cawed, and did not like it if anyone spoke loudly. When the buttermilk-seller shouted from the street, she would cup her ears. The radio could only play in a low hum. She shivered if a vessel fell with a clang. She just could not bear any loud harsh noise.

Appa was short-tempered, and shouted at the slightest excuse. If the chutney was a bit too salty, he would fling the vessel away. Amma's face went red on such days.

Appa's relatives visited us often. When Raji Athai came, Amma would gnash her teeth. As a child, I did not understand why she behaved like that.

Then, Amma would swim her anger and frustration away.

It was wonderful to see her swim. She floated and glided in the water as if she was born and bred in the lake. She moved forward, her arms pushing the water behind, as her beautiful thick hair spread out. There was a strange beauty in her movements. Sometimes she would just float without moving.

I would sit on the bank and watch Amma swim. She swam to the Neeratchiamman temple *mandapam*. There was no one else there. I could see the single dot that was Amma sitting there all alone. Sometimes I feared that she would not return. But soon she would start to swim back. Some women chided her for swimming like this, tirelessly. But she never paid them any heed. After what seemed like a long time, she climbed out of the lake. I would be filled with joy to see her then, her eyes red, saree soaked, and water dripping from her hair. She would gather the washed clothes, still wet, and look at me and smile. Then we slowly walked home together, me grasping her still-wet, ice-cold hand. Drops of water from her hair followed her steps.

The old man sitting on the *thinnai* of the north house in the agraharam would glare at her and mutter under his breath. Amma never looked up. Once home, she changed her clothes, put *tiruneeru*, the sacred ash, on her forehead and dried her hair with *sambirani* smoke. When I think of Amma and try to recall her smell, it is really the fragrance of sambirani that comes to mind.

It was only after I became an adult that I understood that swimming was Amma's only source of joy. Until then, I was really afraid of her.

Amma *had to* swim. Whether she was happy or sad or angry, she would swim. She truly believed that water was her only companion. None of us could really understand Amma.

One night Appa got angry when the household accounts did not tally. From the kitchen, Amma threw the handful of coins that she had with her.

Appa picked them up from the floor.

"You've become insufferable. Can't earn ten rupees, but she's ready to throw a tantrum. Hereafter, if you want money for the household, go ask your father," he yelled.

"Why...drag...*his* name into this?" Her face turned hard.

"For saddling me with a dead weight like you...What's wrong if I drag in his name?"

"You can beat me, you can kick me, but don't you dare even mention his name."

Appa picked up the umbrella and started beating her in a fit of rage. She did not try to resist his blows. He kept on beating her.

"You shameless bitch! You have no place here. Go to your father!"

Amma stood still throughout, her face dry and emotionless. My sister and I stood cowering in a corner. We kept looking at Amma, afraid.

"Go to bed!" Appa shouted at us.

We went to our room and lay down on the mat that was spread for us.

Amma stood in the kitchen, the umbrella lying at her feet. Appa went out to smoke.

After Appa had left, I hesitated for a bit and then called Amma.

"Amma, come, let us go to sleep."

But she would not come. Even when I tugged at her, she did not move.

"You go sleep," she insisted.

I went to bed. I was afraid that she would go away to Thatha's house.

Appa returned after a long time. Amma was nowhere to be found. He came to our room.

"Where is Amma, *da*?"

"We don't know, Appa," my sister said with her eyes half closed.

Appa stepped out of the house with a torch light to search for Amma. She was not in the street. Appa went towards the lake. It was pitch dark and insects chittered in the thick bushes. The tamarind trees metamorphosed into strange forms in the light from the torch.

As Appa had guessed, Amma was swimming in the lake.

In that lonesome lake, in the thick darkness, Amma was swimming by herself.

Appa waved the beam of light and shouted.

"Rukmani...Rukmani!"

Amma began to swim faster towards the Neeratchiamman mandapam as though she did not want the light to touch her.

"Rukku! Rukmani!" Appa kept calling, holding up the torch.

His voice never reached her.

She was soon swallowed by the darkness. There were just two stars in the night sky. The birds which had settled to roost in the trees got agitated by Appa's yelling and flapped their wings. The light from the torch leapt over the dark water like a fish.

Appa did not know what to do. He suppressed his anger and he kept calling her. But she never heard him. We lost sight of her in the darkness. Appa kept waving the torch, not knowing how long he should wait. He returned home, exasperated.

Amma was still not home when we woke up in the morning. Appa was asleep in the easy chair. My sister and I woke him up.

"Your mother is in the lake...go call her," he said and closed his eyes again.

We ran to the lake, and saw her sitting in the mandapam in the centre.

"Amma...Amma!" She did not turn at the sound of our voices. Other people from the agraharam joined us.

"Rukmani...Rukmani!" One after another they called.

A bird turned its head in response to our calls and then swiftly flew away.

Amma went back under the water as though she hated the sound of our voices. Srinivasan, our neighbour from the agraharam, jumped into the lake and started swimming towards the Neeratchiamman mandapam. But he could not find Amma.

What had happened to her? Had she drowned?

Or...had she gone over to the other side?

Srinivasan stood in the mandapam and shouted Amma's name.

Perhaps Amma had decided to live in the water like a mermaid. We were scared—what if she chose not to return?

Srinivasan swam back to the bank, realising that his attempt had been futile.

"Leave her be, she will come back on her own." Appa stood on the bank, staring into the distance.

When will she come? What if she never comes back? We stood there by the lake, terribly afraid.

After a long time we saw her head resurface—her arms were propelling her southwards.

Was she going towards Malayanur? Would she go away to Thatha's house from there?

As my sister and I shouted out her name, Amma slowly disappeared from our sight again.

We kept going back to the lake, again and again, to check. By the evening, the whole town had gathered. Four or five young men swam to her and tried reasoning with her. We could see them talking to her. Still, she would not return.

"Let her die there..." Appa said. He was furious.

No one could make her return.

We stood on the bank and kept shouting but our voices did not reach her. Then Mariammal who worked in the garden heard what happened, and she came to the lake. She jumped in and swam towards Amma. We could see her approach Amma and pull her close. Then the two of them went and sat together in the mandapam.

They were in conversation for a long time.

We thought they would swim back to shore, but that did not happen. Dusk fell and it began to grow dark. The two women kept sitting there in the middle of the lake.

"Amma...!" I shouted. It was a cry of terror from the bottom of my heart.

Neither Amma nor Mariammal paid any heed.

Not certain how long we would have to stand there in the dark, everyone gradually dispersed.

Around ten at night, Mariammal brought Amma home. We did not know what she had said to Amma or how she convinced her to come back.

Mariammal said something to Appa and he kept nodding as she spoke. Then she left.

Amma changed into dry clothes and lit some sambirani to dry and perfume her hair. The fragrance spread all around the house.

My sister and I went and sat next to her. Amma's face looked pale, and in her eyes lay the burden of unutterable grief. She held my hand and drew me close.

"Were you afraid?"

I nodded. Amma pulled my sister close and hugged her. I too held them tight. Her body felt cold, like a pebble that had been under water.

Amma spoke to us calmly, "We are going to Madurai."

"When?" my sister asked.

"Tomorrow."

Within a few days, Appa found a house in Madurai and we settled there. Appa stayed back in the village because of his job.

He would come to Madurai once a week. Within a year, he got transferred to Madurai. Then we sold off the house in Tekkudi. We never went back to the village.

After we moved to Madurai, Amma stopped swimming. She would now bathe in the house. I also noticed another change in her: she had begun to shout at the smallest of things. She, who had once preferred a quiet house, now needed some noise or the other.

Appa stopped fighting with Amma. Sometimes, without any reason, Amma would become angry with Appa and with us, and she would start shouting. She started sleeping in the kitchen at night.

Once we went to visit the temple in Rameswaram and afterwards, to the sea to bathe.

Amma stood on the shore.

"Amma, come. Come, bathe with us in the sea...let's swim together," my sister called out to her.

Amma said, "I don't know how to swim. I'm afraid."

I do not know what Mariammal had told Amma to bring her home that night or what she had told Appa. But one thing was clear: Amma had completely changed after she gave up swimming.

After so many years, my terrified voice calling 'Amma...Amma!' from the dark shore of that lake still echoes in my heart.

Even today Amma remains inscrutable, half-known, half-unknown...like those dark waters.

No One Like Appa

Appa was a strange person.

This is the image of my father that is deeply etched in my heart.

My *thatha*, my grandfather, said that his strangeness was due to the fact that he left home when he was sixteen and wandered around in many places before returning. But that was not the only reason. Appa's nature was like that.

Appa had some qualities not found in anyone else in our family. He loved novelty, he would do anything without inhibition, would dare to try anything, forever unafraid of defeat. Above all, he lived for himself and not for others.

One reads about characters with such admirable qualities in books, but it is not easy to follow these virtues in one's life. Yet Appa did it.

When he was sixteen, Appa had run away from home. He did not take clothes or any cash, just himself. He returned after seven years. Where he had gone and what he had done in those seven years, no one knew. We guessed that he must have lived in many places because he spoke six languages.

Why did he leave home?

Why did he return?

Appa never answered these two questions. Sometimes when we compelled him to answer, he would say: "We must learn many things, and all of them cannot be learnt by staying at home."

What was it that he learnt by running away? No one knew. But it was the world outside that had shaped his courage.

When he returned, he was twenty-three and Thatha was determined to get him married at once. Appa agreed, subject to some conditions.

"No one must come with me when I go to meet the girl. You can talk to her family only if I like the girl. The marriage must be conducted in a library."

Thatha was angry and called it idiocy. Appa firmly stated that if these conditions were not accepted, he would not get married.

The family had no option but to agree, since they knew how stubborn Appa was. One early morning, he cycled to the girl's house in the neighbouring village alone. The girl's family was not informed that he would come. They were completely taken aback to see him at six o'clock in the morning. Moreover, they were amused to see his unkempt look, sporting a thick beard and wearing a three-fourth sleeve shirt and *veshti*.

He asked the girl's family for a towel and soap to have a bath. He must have been the first man to ask the family of the prospective bride for such things.

He drew water from the well and had his bath. He went in drying his hair and ate *idli*s at their place. He then told them about himself.

"I am not working anywhere presently, and I don't intend to work... There are many things in this world that we must know. We should first learn about them. Isn't it a shame that we do not know the names of the stars in the sky? I have learnt about them, and now that I have returned, I am going to test what I have learnt...Please do not depend on me or expect me to earn for the family."

The girl's family was stunned on hearing this. They had agreed to this alliance only because my grandfather owned lands and a house.

Amma was sixteen years old then. Appa gave her a post card, asking her to post it if she liked him.

On the sixth day the card arrived with just one word, "No."

Appa read that card again and again. He even examined the letters through a magnifying glass.

A girl did not like him. She disliked something she saw in him. But he liked the girl! So he vowed to make her understand him. With this in mind, he decided to cycle around in front of her house.

At our village annual fair, there would be a man who rode the cycle day and night in the same spot. He would ride non-stop for nine days without getting off the bicycle. He bathed while riding, he ate and slept while riding... At the end of nine days, the man collected a hefty earning and went home. Appa tried the same trick to win his bride.

Amma was very embarrassed that he was cycling in front of her house. She was too shy to even come out and see him. Appa, like the trained acrobat, took a pot of water and poured it over himself while cycling. He had food on a plate, drank soda—all while cycling. He did not stop even during the night. On the third day, early in the morning, Amma peeped out secretly and he was there cycling with gusto. When he saw her, he began cycling even faster, and that made Amma smile.

She liked his stubbornness and his never-say-die attitude. While riding he made a paper bird and let it fly towards her. The tiny paper bird fell at her feet. Amma picked it up and quietly went inside.

By the next day Amma had agreed to marry him. But her parents did not agree to conduct the marriage in the library. So it was conducted in her house. On the morning of the wedding, Appa did something startling—he shaved his head.

Everyone was upset that the bridegroom had shaved his head. But Amma smiled. Her smile affirmed that she liked his appearance.

The marriage was a simple ceremony. Appa read out what he had written on a piece of paper.

"I will not beat my wife.

"I will never make a demand for money or property from her family.

"I will educate her.

"I will have only two children.

"I will not ask her to attach my name to hers...

There were ten such statements. No one had ever heard of a bridegroom giving such assurances to the bride's family. Amma's relatives made fun of him. But Appa never broke any of his vows.

Two days after the marriage, Appa began teaching Amma to ride a cycle. Appa sat behind Amma as she rode the cycle, and the whole village watched the scene.

Then he ordered that the front door of the house should never be locked. At night it would be shut but not locked. If we ever left town, he would hang a notice in front of the door, but it was never locked with a key.

It was Appa who always made breakfast at home. Amma only made lunch. We just had fruits at night. That was the routine.

Appa was the only person who knew every beggar in town by name. During festivals, our house would be full of beggars. Appa gave them new clothes and fed them good food.

One day Appa brought a telescope and placed it on the terrace. He showed us all the stars that could be seen in the sky. Anyone could come and look at the stars with that telescope, it was not just for his family, he announced. But no one availed of the offer. Two months later he gifted it to a government school.

He kept two chairs outside the house. Anybody could sit there and read the papers. In fact, he ate his meals sitting in a chair outside, in full view of the people who went by.

"What is there to hide when we eat? Does any beast in this world eat behind closed doors?" He ate his meals in front of everyone to show that he had no reason to eat secretly. He made others eat openly too.

He lit up the stove with energy from sunlight, generated electricity with the cycle dynamo and made a simple motor to draw water from the well mechanically. He would use household waste to make fuel. He constructed a floating garden by potting plants in empty powder tins and Amul tins. He even made ornaments from outdated coins.

He made another small motor to draw water from the village pond and have it flow to the temple. He made a spray hose to bathe the temple elephant. He made various types of paper birds to delight children. Appa made us believe that there was nothing impossible for him.

People thought that what Appa did was madness. Many made fun of him, called him a crackpot. But Amma believed he was a wise person who thought independently. She did not stop him from doing anything. Even when his experiments resulted in loss of money and property, she did not hold him back or scold him. She trusted him implicitly and completely.

When I was born, his first child, a son, Appa named me Sophia. Everyone on Thatha's side of the family objected to giving a boy a girl's name.

"Names are neutral. I don't believe in distinguishing them as boy's names and girl's names," Appa responded.

He named my sister Solar. In school and other public places, we were teased because of our names. Appa told us firmly that we should ignore it.

As he had vowed, Appa let Amma study what she wished. Amma completed M.A. degrees in Tamil, History and English through correspondence courses. Then she began working as a clerk in a co-operative bank.

He asked everyone living on his street to make one extra *dosai* or idli every day. Then he collected these and gave them away to those who were hungry. He called this "Dosai Thittam" or the Dosai Plan.

Once we went to Kanyakumari, riding a bicycle each. This must have been the first time a whole family was seen going for a seven-day vacation by cycle. Wherever we went, we spoke with strangers and stayed with them for the night. We ate whatever they offered.

After we returned, Appa wondered if he could take everyone in our village on a trip like this. How nice it would be! But that was not to happen.

Later, he wanted to get us admitted to the popular St. Xavier School. So he took a sheet with ten questions to the headmaster and asked him to answer them. The headmaster read the questions. Then he folded the sheet, put it on the table and placed a paperweight on it.

"Your son is not the only student in our school. This school has been here for sixty years. Thousands of students have studied here. Don't worry. We will take care..."

Appa smiled as he realised he would not get the answers he was looking for. He then gave the headmaster a notebook.

"I must know what the teacher teaches every day. Education is not your job alone, we too share half the responsibility. We will teach our child at home. You and I will teach the children jointly."

The headmaster was annoyed by his idea. He told Appa that such stupid plans cannot be implemented.

In that case, Appa said, he did not want to put his child in that school. He then enrolled me in the Government Elementary School. In truth it was only Appa himself who taught us. He set apart two hours of his day just for this. He taught us maths and science in an innovative way. He also insisted that we learn new languages, and he taught us Chinese, French, Hindi and Urdu. He taught us everything—swimming, carpentry, pottery and so on.

Sometimes he looked like a clown. But Appa never cared much about his looks.

He cut our hair himself. He whitewashed our house. He cleaned the well. Once a year he took us all on a vacation to somewhere far away. He discussed everything under the sun with us.

He stayed with us till his fiftieth year. Then he called us one day and said, "I have stayed at home for too long. I think this has been enough. I am leaving."

No one asked him where he planned to go. He just said, "There is a world outside the house too."

It was sad to think of the house without Appa. But he was never one to worry about how others felt about him, their sadness or pain.

One day he went to the provision store to buy sugar and did not come back. Around six in the evening, a sales boy from the store came to our house and handed over the sugar and the change to us.

Appa had left. We did not know where he went. But we understood that he was moving in the direction that his heart wanted to go.

We did not search for him. We started to live independently like him. On some days, all of a sudden, thoughts of him would rise and burst inside. At those times, memories of Appa would swamp us with sorrow.

Appa never got tired of this world. In some corner of this earth at this very moment, he must be helping someone understand the meaning of life. That is what gave him happiness.

Now tell me, is there anyone like Appa but him?

The Dolls with No Eyebrows

The incident that happened at Hassan Shikari's house was very strange and almost unbelievable. But truth, they say, is stranger than fiction. Often, things that occur in reality may not be found even in stories.

We do not pay attention to mysterious events until they have happened. And after that we begin to wonder how they happened. The truth is that these wonders, mysteries or miracles occur to remind us that this world is not entirely under our control. The Hassan Shikari incident is one like that.

So what really happened at Hassan Shikari's house?

The two dolls arrived together.

And what is so wondrous about that, you may ask?

That is because you do not know the story of the two dolls.

These were two white porcelain dolls made in China. It seems they were given as wedding gifts to Hassan. These were hand-painted dolls. One was a man, the other a woman. The male doll had a round cap, a knotted kerchief around its neck and a small belt on its waist. The woman doll wore a red gown; its left hand was visible, while the right was hidden inside the gown, and its hair curled in the front like a crescent. Neither doll had eyebrows. It gave them an unusual appearance. The expression on their faces was astonishingly lifelike, a testament to the doll maker's mastery as a craftsman.

Hassan's wife said that the dolls were a married pair. Though they looked like ordinary dolls, there was a strange anecdote about them: if one doll got separated from the other somehow, they would miraculously join each other again.

How could inanimate dolls do that, you ask? Maybe like human beings, dolls too are ruled by destiny. The strange thing was that these dolls would re-unite no matter in what way they were separated. But this had not been tested by the Hassan household yet.

Hassan Shikari is a silk merchant. His family went to Burma from India for business. It was their ancestral trade. One of his ancestors had gone to China to procure silk. The trade relation that began then continued for generations down till Hassan Shikari. He is now eighty-six, but even today he goes to watch his shop running with keen interest. Although nowadays he does not go to China to procure silk, they buy it from Kashmir. Hassan would explain with regret that ever since artificial silk entered the market, real silk had receded to the background.

The dolls were gifted by the Chinese merchant and family friend Kwen Lee when Hassan Shikari got married, at eighteen years of age. Kwen Lee's wife was Indian. When he gave Hassan the dolls, he did not utter a word about the strange secret behind them. Three months later he came to tell Hassan about the floods in the river Irrawaddy.

"These dolls cannot be separated. They are an inseparable couple. By chance if one is parted from the other, they will re-join."

"It is hard for people who get separated to find each other. And you want me to believe this tall story about dolls?" Hassan scoffed.

"No, I speak the truth. Such dolls are no longer made. Four centuries ago, the bride's parents gave dolls like these as wedding gifts. It was a Chinese custom. The dolls I gifted you are four hundred years old. They have been preserved and handed down by my family as precious heirlooms. Out of love I gave them to you," Kwen Lee said in a firm voice.

When she heard this, Hassan's wife grew very fond of the dolls. She wiped them clean, and placed them on the shelf next to their bed. The pair was so well-behaved too. The wife doll's cheeks were pink and smooth like rose petals.

"Kwen Lee is right. These dolls are really strange," Hassan's wife said one day.

"Why? What happened?"

"The two dolls turn away in embarrassment whenever we make love."

"Impossible! Dolls can't feel shy. Why would they turn?"

"Perhaps even dolls do not want to invade someone's privacy."

"How peculiar! Tell me what happened."

"I have been seeing this for the last few days. During the day they stand facing our bed, but at night they turn away by themselves."

"All lies! I'll hug you tight right now. Let me see if the dolls turn away."

"Ayyo! Is this the time for love-making?" She pushed Hassan away. The dolls stood still, motionless.

At night, before going to bed, Hassan looked at the dolls to confirm that they were looking towards the bed. When he woke up early next morning and switched on the light...the dolls...the dolls had their backs to him! Strange! He woke up his wife to tell her that it was true: the dolls turned away to give them privacy during their intimate moments.

"So do you believe me now? These dolls are observing us."

"Do you think they can hear what we speak?"

"I don't know. But I do think that they can experience feelings. Your friend is right, they are not ordinary dolls."

Not wanting the dolls in her bedroom, Hassan Shikari's wife moved them to the showcase in the hall. For twelve years, they remained there and were not parted from each other.

"The dolls have not aged at all; they have the same smile, the same youthful appearance and the same shining blue eyes. Only we have grown old," Hassan's wife said one day.

"It seems as if we were married just yesterday, but I feel tired and bored."

"If you are tired of family life, why don't you go to the forest? Why do you keep hanging around the bedroom?" Hassan's wife taunted him, pretending to be angry.

"Shamima, the dolls do not fight like we do. Ageing is a gift given to human beings; age is our guide, our teacher. But for you, age has made you so impertinent. The Shamima I married was a quiet girl," Hassan teased her.

"This was born of association with you," she replied playfully.

Hassan Shikari thought they were as happy a couple as the dolls.

During the Second World War, bombs rained on Rangoon and they had to vacate the house to go away to India one night. In all this tumult, Hassan Shikari somehow forgot the male doll.

When they reached India by ship, only the female doll was in the bamboo box they had packed it in. Hassan's wife was very upset at losing the male doll, but she did not show it.

They bought a house in Lucknow thereafter. The female doll stood alone in their drawing room. Six years later, a waste-paper man came to Hassan's house to buy old newspapers and empty bottles. A short while after the man had left, Hassan's younger son said that he had found the male doll.

Hassan Shikari could not believe his eyes. The male doll lay on the floor in a corner, all dusty and dirty.

How did it come there?

Did the old waste-paper man bring it?

Why did he leave it there?

Hassan's wife was in tears when she saw the doll. She picked it up lovingly, wiped it with her sari and placed it near the female doll.

She thought the male doll was looking at its doll wife with yearning in its eyes.

"See? After so many years and after roaming all over the country, in the end it has come right back to us. Hereafter we must never let them leave one another," she said.

Hassan was very happy too. In fact he was filled with hope that all the wealth he had lost will be regained.

He dusted the dolls himself. And every day before leaving for his shop, he would stand near the dolls for a minute and utter something to himself.

All the guests who came to Hassan Shikari's house looked at the dolls with wonder when they heard the story. A police officer's wife asked Hassan if he would sell the dolls to her. He refused very firmly.

One summer Hassan went to Nainital with his family. When they returned, the dolls were not to be seen. One of the servants had stolen them. Hassan Shikari lodged a police complaint. He threatened the servants, but the dolls could not be found. The loss affected him very deeply, and in the weeks that followed, he fell very ill.

The dolls appeared in his dream one night. He moaned and sighed for them even in his sleep. He spent a lot of money to find them. He even posted an advertisement in the papers. But the dolls were nowhere to be found.

Six months after this happened, a railway porter brought the dolls and gave them to Hassan. He said he had found them in a railway carriage. One foot of the male doll had chipped. Hassan wept with joy, unable to believe that the dolls had come back to him. He gave the porter two thousand rupees as reward.

He decided that the dolls should not be displayed outside. He had a wooden box made for them. He placed the dolls inside that and put them away in the locker where he kept his money. Every day when he opened the locker to take out money, he also took the dolls out and bowed to them. Then he would place them inside again and lock the safe.

Hassan Shikari's eldest daughter-in-law was childless for a long time. This was often discussed by everyone in the family as if it was a big problem. Vexed at the family members because of this, the daughter-in-law vented her anger on the dolls by taking them out from the locker one day and throwing them in the dustbin. Hassan Shikari could not bear this and fell down in a faint. When his wife found out that the perpetrator of this act was the eldest daughter-in-law, she chased her out of the house. The daughter-in-law refused to tell what she did with the dolls.

Three years later, one summer, as the well was being dredged, they found the two dolls. The colours had faded and they were covered in mud. Once they were washed clean and held up, the blue eyes shone, as calm as always.

Hassan Shikari's daughter-in-law heard about the recovery of the dolls. "I threw them in the dustbin. How did they end up in the well? Baffling!"

It remained a mystery who threw the dolls down the well.

After this Hassan did not part from the dolls and always kept them close to him. Even if his grandchildren asked, he would not give them the dolls. When he was unwell and in the hospital, the dolls were next to his bed.

The day Hassan underwent heart surgery, one doll went missing. It was the female doll. The family decided not to upset him with the truth, so they told him that the doctor had asked them to take the dolls away back to the house.

"Where are the dolls?" was Hassan's first question when he returned home from the hospital.

They brought him the male doll. He glared at every one, but said nothing.

"Wherever she is, she will come searching for you," he told the doll before him.

But it did not happen. Every morning when he saw the male doll, he wished that by nightfall the female doll would be found. But that did not happen. Every night he went to sleep with a heavy heart. As days went by without the doll being found, Hassan behaved just like a father searching for his lost daughter. And he wept.

Seven years and thirty-six days later, the female doll suddenly appeared at his doorstep, its hand broken. Nobody knew who left it there or how it arrived. He was not keen to know the details either.

He held the doll with the broken hand, and began wailing—why had this happened? Seeing him cry, his wife too wept.

Next morning, he decorated the female doll with ornaments and placed it next to the male one. He gave a feast to celebrate the reunion of the dolls. The guests were astonished on hearing the incredible the story of the dolls.

"They must have been a man and woman who could not unite in their lifetime. That is why after they became dolls, they cannot be parted," said a girl who came for the feast as she looked at the dolls. Hassan Shikari felt she was right.

One night Hassan's wife suffered a cardiac arrest and died before they could take her to the hospital. The dolls were the only solace for the grieving Hassan now. He kept them near his pillow.

To comfort himself he would talk to them every day, telling them about his wife's love and their happy days together. It seemed as if a pall of sadness covered the dolls' faces.

One night, as Hassan was telling the dolls about how his wife behaved when they were newly married, the female doll who was on the bed fell down and shattered. Flustered, Hassan Shikari bent down towards the floor, when he saw the male doll throw itself from the bed.

The two dolls with no eyebrows now lay in pieces on the floor.

Hassan Shikari started crying loudly.

He had not cried like this even when his wife died.

Gandhi on Their Shoulders

The car was tearing through the dense fog. There were five men in the car. Two were Indian, and the other three were Ugandan. The youngest was the driver. His name was Mwanga, he was about eighteen. But he was sturdy and over six feet tall. His face looked as if it was cast in stone, and he drove like a robot.

They were heading towards the river Nile which flowed through Jinja district next to Busoga in eastern Uganda. They had started from Kampala by road. The two Indian passengers were elderly men who had settled down in Uganda more than thirty years ago. Naresh Gidwani must have been over seventy; he wore a white *khadi* cap, and kurta pyjama in the same white khadi. He had a wide forehead and a full head of thick, grey hair. He wore large spectacles that did not suit his face. Shukla, the other Indian, was around sixty. He was short with a big paunch, hooked nose and dark lips. He too wore khadi. He had a wooden box on his lap which he held with great care. Shukla and Gidwani did not talk with each other. It seemed as if they were together only to carry out a responsibility entrusted to them. The car proceeded at a moderate pace.

In the second half of the nineteenth century, Sikhs were brought to Uganda as labourers. They constructed the Ugandan railway network from Mombasa to Kisumu in 1901 and in Kampala around 1931 with the help of Alibhai Mulla Jeevanjee, the Imperial British contractor. In this arduous task of laying the railway track, some Indians lost their limbs and many others lost their lives. Once the track was laid and the work was over, some families returned to India while others decided to remain in Uganda. Besides these people some Gujaratis who were cloth merchants became permanent residents there. Some of them raised money for India's freedom struggle and also ran a journal for private circulation among the Indians.

Charlie who was in the front seat was about fifty. He had curly hair, a split lower lip, a scar from a cut over his eyebrow and large ears. He had worked for some time in the postal department and therefore had good relations with Indians. His was a large family—he had two wives and nine children. He wished to visit India once, mainly because he found Indian women beautiful. He was particularly attracted to their round faces—he noticed this among the Indian women who lived in Uganda—and the way they draped their sarees. Obade, who sat next to Charlie, was a young man who had dropped out of college midway. He was keenly interested in football and spent his days drinking. Before he got into the car, Charlie had warned him sternly not to drink. Obade had a small bottle tucked away in his pocket, but he did not take it out. He never asked the purpose of this trip to the Nile. It irritated him, but he had agreed to come at Charlie's insistence. Charlie wanted him along because he could row in the river.

"How much longer to go?" Gidwani had a fixed stare.

"It will take two hours," Charlie replied.

"The car is moving so slowly, like a hearse. At this rate it will be afternoon when we reach the river," Obade said. He was clearly fed up.

"This *is* a hearse," said Shukla.

Obade looked uncomprehendingly at Charlie.

"Why are we really going to the Nile? For what purpose?"

"We must immerse the ashes in the river. You have to row the boat, that is your job," Charlie replied.

"I am famished. And my head is splitting. Travelling with old people is like guarding a dead cow, very boring!" Obade said.

"Everyone grows old. When you grow old, you will know the pain of old age."

"We do not bother about ageing. Counting the years is the white man's trick. As long as the blood that courses through our veins is warm, we are young," Charlie said.

"We are like clouds. Clouds are eternally young. Except for us human beings, no other living creature counts its age," Obade said in agreement.

"That is not true. Even the trees age, and we calculate it by their rings," Gidwani said.

"Indians like arithmetic, huh?" Charlie smirked.

"One, two, three, four...after that it is all a crowd. It is enough if you can count that much." Obade laughed.

"Stop laughing and be quiet for a while," Shukla chided them.

The car went over a bump on the road and the box on his lap wobbled. He hugged it tight as though it were his child.

"Does this box contain the remains of a dead man?" Obade asked.

"Mahatma Gandhi's *asthi,* his ashes," replied Gidwani.

"Who is he? Your father?" Obade wanted to know.

"No. The Father of India. Millions of Indians called him their father," Shukla replied.

"How can one man be the father of the whole of India?" Obade was perplexed.

"He was *like* a father. That word stands for responsibility, it means giving love without expecting anything in return. You think of Christ as a father too, don't you?" asked Shukla.

"He was God," Charlie said.

"Gandhi was a godlike man," replied Shukla.

"Why do you want to immerse a dead man's ashes in the river?" Obade asked.

"After he dies, a man belongs to the entire world, and by immersing his ashes in different important rivers, we are entrusting him to the world. As long as these rivers flow, his memories will remain," Shukla said.

"Rivers have no memories," Obade remarked.

"The river writes down its memories on pebbles," Charlie added.

"You spoke the truth. It is the pebbles that hold the river's memories," said Gidwani.

"Did Gandhi ever see the Nile?" Obade asked.

"No. Only his ashes will know the river."

"Strange. A river he has not seen in his lifetime, he will know after his life," Charlie said.

"He was killed in Delhi. His last rites were performed there. A friend of the Gandhi family, Vilas Mehta, had originally received it. He arranged for special prayers and for the ashes to be brought to South Africa by sea. We received the ashes from him and have been bidden to immerse them in the Nile. Not just here, parts of his ashes have been immersed in rivers and seas all over the world," said Gidwani.

"Have you seen Gandhi?" Charlie asked.

The car turned at a curve where a woman was walking with two dogs on leash. Far away one could see a small village with low-roofed huts. Ugandan villages looked just like Indian ones.

"I have seen him in photographs. I don't even know what his voice sounds like," replied Shukla.

"You are carrying on your lap the ashes of Gandhi whom you have never even seen once. Do you feel Gandhi's weight?" Obade asked.

"Gandhi is now weightless."

"You cannot assign a value to the ashes. A man who is dead can achieve things that a living man cannot. Do not underestimate the dead," Charlie said.

"That is very true. Death marks the end of a person's physical life, his body, but his good deeds continue to live for a very long time. A man does not die as long as there is someone adhering to his principles, keeping his thoughts and deeds alive. Gandhi was such a man." Shukla's words were emphatic.

"What did Gandhi do for India?" asked Obade.

"He was the one who identified ethics, love and *ahimsa* or nonviolence as basic Indian virtues. He was the only voice of the Indian conscience. Has any other leader in this world, who is worshipped by millions, cleaned his own toilet? Or lived a simple life wearing just a cloth to cover himself waist down? Or spun the yarn himself for his khadi clothes? The methods and weapons he chose for battle were erstwhile unknown in India. He made love the weapon of war, and the British rulers were afraid to face that. His voice was always the voice of the simple, ordinary people. Mahatma Gandhi's struggle actually began here, in South Africa. He fought against racism and was put in jail."

Obade's expression changed at this.

"Was he black?"

"Black, but an Indian," said Shukla.

"How did he fight a battle without lifting a weapon?" Charlie was surprised.

"Ahimsa was his way," Gidwani said.

Mwanga who had been silently driving the car all this time asked in a soft voice, "He was not a Messiah, was he?"

"Did not the Messiah too appear as a man?" replied Gidwani.

"How did Gandhi die? Was he unwell?" Mwanga asked.

"No. He was shot dead," Shukla said.

"By an Englishman?" asked Obade.

"No, it was an Indian who shot him," Shukla sighed sorrowfully.

"Strange. Why should an Indian kill the father of their nation?"

"It is beyond our comprehension too," Gidwani said.

"He was killed on his way to offer prayers. Even his assassin folded his hands in a *namaste* before he lifted the gun."

"Why did the murderer salute him like that?" Obade did not understand.

"Wasn't Gandhi his father too?" Shukla said softly.

"I am filled with sorrow to hear this. Good men are killed unjustly. The same thing happened to Jesus too," Mwanga said.

Shukla tried to say something but was unable to speak, and his eyes brimmed with tears. Charlie must have noted that; he gestured to Obade to keep quiet.

The car proceeded at a slow pace and Mwanga who was driving asked, "Do you have a photo of the Mahatma? I want to see it."

"Sure, I'll show it to you when we reach the river," said Shukla.

"The river Nile was formed because a god once lied. You know that, don't you?" asked Charlie.

"I have never heard that story. What is it?" Gidwani asked.

"Yes, there is a story about the Nile. The Greek god Zeus had a beautiful wife called Hera. It was impossible to hide anything from her. One day Zeus met a lovely young girl called Io and fell in love with her. He tried many cunning tricks and told many lies to keep this from his wife, but all was in vain. When Hera found out, she drove Io away to the desert. It rained torrentially because Zeus who had until that day never spoken untruth had lied. It rained and rained for years and the water formed a huge lake. This water then turned into a river that flowed through the desert for the sake of Io. That river is the Nile," Charlie narrated.

"Every river holds an interesting story like this, no?" Shukla asked.

"There are no rivers without a story. Aren't raindrops the tears shed by God?" asked Mwanga.

"Why does God weep?" asked Gidwani.

"At man's actions. Why else?" answered Mwanga.

"Gandhi did not stop shedding tears at what men did. He strived to wipe away all sorrow. Gandhi pervaded all over India like air. His simplicity was his strength."

"I am filled with respect for him after listening to you," said Mwanga.

"Like you, we too began loving him without ever having seen him. We walked his path and did what he said. His death has completely shaken us."

"Gandhi should not have been killed," Mwanga said solemnly.

"They are trying to bury his principles and values along with him. That is worrying," Gidwani said.

"I'm really worried about what will happen to India now," said Shukla.

"The only hope is Nehru. But he will not be given a free hand," said Gidwani.

"Gandhi is irreplaceable. Till now he was with us in reality, and henceforth he will be with us as a guiding light."

"Well said. Gandhi is truly a light, and light belongs to all. Each country does not have a separate light of its own, does it?" asked Gidwani.

After this no one spoke. The car drove towards the riverhead. They parked the car at a suitable spot and started walking. They could see a row of habitations along the river bank.

Mwanga asked if he could carry the box with the ashes. Shukla paused for a moment. Then he transferred it to Mwanga's shoulders.

"We are carrying Gandhi," said Charlie.

They walked in silence.

"Gandhi's ashes must be heavier than his body. Because it holds the tears of millions of Indians," Shukla said.

Mwanga carried the ashes till the river. Obade arranged for a boat. When it came they sailed down the Nile in the boat. The foaming river with its billowing viridescent waters looked like the fierce sea. The boat rocked because of the strong current.

They stopped the boat in the middle of the river, and Shukla took out a bronze vessel from the wooden box. He touched the vessel and placed his fingers on his eyes in respect. Charlie, Gidwani and Mwanga each paid their respects too. They immersed the bronze vessel with the ashes in the water. Some of the ash flew out because of the wind and got into Mwanga's eyes. He did not wipe it away. Gandhi merged with the waters of the Nile, the world's longest river. The Nile which has seen many rulers and kingdoms carried the Mahatma too in itself.

As they returned Mwanga rued painfully, "It is a grievous sin to kill the father. Your country will not be let off lightly."

"Only the Mahatma can protect India," said Shukla, his face dark with apprehension.

Far away from a tree came a bird's cry, as though in affirmation.

Gauthama's Dreams

Two days before his death, Gauthama Buddha had two dreams. Both were about events that had happened in his life. He did not know why they recurred as dreams. Maybe his mind had not released itself fully from the past, he thought.

The dreams were so clear it felt like the events were happening right before his eyes. Why should they be called dreams then? Hadn't these things happened in his life, in reality? That he spoke to his stepmother was true. That she replied was also true. Except, in his dream, this conversation took place in the sky. His stepmother was sleeping amidst the clouds, and he too stood beneath a cloud.

How strange! Gauthama could not forget the dreams. He kept searching for their meaning. These two dreams that he could not discuss with anyone else he buried deep inside him.

The First Dream

Siddhartha asked his stepmother, "Mitra says that my birth itself is a dream. Is it true?"

Prajagothami, the junior queen of Kapilavasthu, was reclining on a cloud-bed. The flowers in her hair seemed to be peeping at her face. Her long tresses were spread out like the tributaries of a dark river. Two of her maids were waving fans above her head. Their hands were moving right and left, evenly, like an automaton.

Prajagothami looked affectionately at Gauthama standing in front of her.

"Not just yours, Gauthama. All our births are someone's dream, aren't they?"

"Not like that. Mitra says I appeared in my mother's dream before I was born. That is what I am asking about."

"Not an ordinary dream, Gauthama. It was a strange dream that your mother Mayadevi had. An elephant, and that too a white elephant with six ivory tusks, appeared in her dream. Its ears glowed a brilliant blue. The world had never seen a tusker like that. It was a flying elephant with a golden head. Yes. Then that weightless animal came towards her, light as a raindrop, floating down to earth, softly, entrancingly. The elephant laughed—she could never forget the laughter. A soundless laughter. Yes, Gauthama, it was a laughter made of light, of pure radiance. That elephant whispered in your mother's ear, 'Maya, will you receive me?' Maya opened her arms wide with joy. Just as the fragrance of a joss-stick enters one's nostrils and brings about a sense of elation, the elephant entered her, diffused within her and disappeared. Then, you were born."

"Mother, am I a flying elephant? Can I fly too?"

"Yes, my son. You too will fly away. Not today. But another day, you will leave this palace, this country and fly away to places far, far away. Gauthama, these forests, mountains, rivers and this country are all yours. Tomorrow you will rule over them. Mitra is an innocent girl. She is just teasing you."

"When I talk with Mitra, many questions form in my mind, I am able to see many wonders. Mother, why is Mitra a girl?'

"She was born a girl, so she is a girl. What kind of a question is that?"

"Why was *I* not born a girl?"

"No, Siddha, you don't need the misery suffered by a girl."

"Do you suffer too, mother?"

"Not just me, there is no woman in this world who has not suffered pain."

"Mitra says the same thing. 'Brother, try to understand girls like me some day.' But...I understand Mitra very well already, mother."

"No, my son. No man can ever understand a woman fully. How can a person who only wants to drink water understand the nature of water?"

"Amma, when you speak, you are always looking at something in the distance. What do you see there so far away?"

"Gauthama, from the day you were born, my mind looks only at the distance, to the future. Your future has already begun to sound like distant thunder in my ears. Go play, Gauthama, play happily. Enjoy all the pleasures of life now while you can. Later in your life, you won't be able to experience these joys."

Gauthama was filled with confusion and kept looking at Prajagothami's face. The cloud began to dissolve like bubbles in water. In front of his eyes, his stepmother and her attendants started disappearing like smoke. And he felt as if he was falling from the sky.

He was falling headlong to the earth when he woke up with a start.

Dream. Yes, a dream.

What kind of a dream was that...?

Gauthama kept thinking about it. Suddenly the memories of his childhood, the palace and his stepmother's love gushed in. He sighed deeply with regret.

The Second Dream

In the garden called Upavanam, fountains sprang and water flowed as incessantly as a child talking to himself. Somewhere in the garden a parrot cried. Siddhartha followed the sound in search of the bird. The parrot flew and sat on another tree and squawked, as if it was playing hide-and-seek with him.

"Parrot, parrot, what are you saying and to whom?" Siddhartha asked.

"Neither to you, nor to me. Parrots rejoice in talking to themselves," came the answer.

Siddhartha was puzzled. He looked around to see who had spoken. A young boy was standing under the cotton tree.

"Who are you? How did you come here?" Siddhartha asked.

"I came the same way that these parrots did. My name is Mara."

"Did you give the guards the slip and enter?" Siddhartha was surprised.

"Won't the people who let parrots enter allow little boys too?"

"Parrots fly in."

"So did I."

"You are no parrot."

"Who says only parrots can fly?" Mara laughed.

"Why, I am unable to fly. I have tried many times."

"If you don't find your wings how would you fly?"

"Do human beings have wings?"

"Of course..."

"Where are they?"

"You have to find them."

"Have you found yours?"

"I came to this Upavanam to find them."

"Does your father work in the palace?"

"He can do a thousand jobs. He might have worked in the palace as well."

"Mara, why are these parrots chattering incessantly? What are they talking about?"

"Just like you and I, the parrots chatter."

"What makes parrots happy?" Siddhartha wanted to know.

"Let us ask the parrots themselves."

"Do you speak the parrots' tongue?"

"I can talk to parrots, trees, squirrels—everything. Why, I can even speak to water."

"That's surprising! How is it possible for you?"

"It is possible even for you."

"But I don't know their language."

"You can learn. It is easy."

"Will you teach me?"

"I will. And what will you give me in return?"

"Ask me for whatever you want."

"You must come with me wherever I call you."

"Out of this palace?"

"Yes, you must come to a distant land far from this palace and this country, across forests and rivers."

"What is there?"

"You will know when you reach there."

"They will not permit me to leave this palace."

"Even parrots can go out of this palace and return. Poor you, you are like this lemon tree, unable to move from its spot."

"Mara, your words hide something."

"No. I want to show you everything, one by one. This palace keeps many matters out of your sight. I am going to show them all to you."

"I am the prince. They do not hide anything from me."

"The world you see is not the truth. You do not know the truth. You remain hidden behind veils."

"You are trying to confuse me by saying this and that. What are the parrots talking about? Ask them and tell me."

"Brother, I will tell you right away."

Mara made some parrot-like noises. The very next moment, a parrot replied. Mara squawked again. The parrot replied once more.

"There is nothing new in this palace, says the parrot," Mara said with a smile.

"What did you say to it?"

"I said there is nothing new in this world. The parrot agreed with me and said 'yes, yes.'"

Gauthama was filled with confusion.

"Tell me the truth. Who are you?"

"I am you. Or you can say I am your desire."

"Will my desire assume a form?"

"Not all desires take forms. But some do."

"This is very confusing!"

"The fire is a form that desire assumes. That is why it is always flickering."

"Mara, what you say scares me. Who are you? A *yaksha*?"

"Not an ordinary yaksha, a *maha* yaksha."

He closed his fist and opened it again. There was a flame on his palm. "This fire will not burn you. Touch it and see."

Gauthama touched it with hesitation. It did not burn his finger.

"How does it feel?" Mara asked.

"It is like touching a bird."

"Did you say 'a bird'? You are right. The fire *is* a bird. We will let it fly."

Before he finished speaking, Mara flung the fire in his hand high up in the sky. The fire flew up to the sky like a posse of fireflies. Still wondering, Siddhartha turned around, but Mara was nowhere to be seen.

Where did Mara go?

Perhaps he had flown away like the parrots.

The fire of desire. A captivating fire. A fire that can fly away like a bird.

As Siddhartha kept thinking of it, he felt a sense of deep yearning.

Suddenly he heard a loud laugh. It was Mara's voice...

"Siddhartha, desire never dies. It is fire. It may disappear temporarily, but it will definitely re-appear."

Gauthama woke up with a start to realise that he had been dreaming and found his disciples sleeping around him. He sat up and ruminated over the dreams of the last two days.

What are these dreams?

What do they mean?

He closed his eyes in meditation. Then as a realisation dawned on him, he sat calmly in peace.

The dreams did not come to him again.

He was alive...for just one more day.

The Man Who Walked Backwards

When I was thirteen, my Perippa, my father's elder brother—his name was Mayilvahanam—suddenly started walking backwards. He did not tell anyone why he began to do this. When the whole world was walking forwards, Mayilvahanam Perippa was the only one who walked backwards, his arms swinging by his side.

All the people in the town gaped at him, wondering what kind of lunacy this was. Perippa always wore a white shirt and white trousers. I have never seen a spot of dirt on his clothes. He moved backwards as though he wanted to have nothing to do with the rest of the hustling and bustling world, constantly moving forward.

When he walked past my school walking backwards from home, I would see him and wonder how he did this so effortlessly without knocking against anyone.

When my classmates called him a "loosu", a madman, I was filled with anger. Was it wrong to walk backwards? Apart from his walking, in what way did Perippa behave strangely? He ate like the rest of us, went to work, read magazines in the library, went to the temple... the only difference was the way he walked...which was, well, backwards.

It was a habit he had adopted on his own. His wife, Indrani Perimma, was a short-tempered woman and detested Perippa's craziness.

It was impossible to change two things about Mayilvahanam Perippa. One, he brought home total strangers to feed them. How he found these starving people nobody knows. Itinerants, beggars, travellers, blind mendicants, *boomboom maattukaaran* and *kudukuduppaikaaran*—tribal fortunetellers—he brought all of them home. Perimma shouted at him when he asked her to cook and serve this ragged lot, but he cared not a bit. Many people have eaten at their house, including North Indians who did not know any Tamil.

His other habit was to keep on reading regardless of the complaints made against him by his family. Every day, he brought three books from the library and read them. If Perimma picked a quarrel, he would begin to read out loudly. That was his only way of venting. Once Perimma had snatched the book from his hand and thrown it in the fire. He did not get angry. He picked up another book and started reading it aloud. Perimma asked him why he read books like a man possessed, and if it would fetch him any wealth. Perippa silenced her, saying that she knew nothing about such things.

He could never fight with anyone and that is what made him vulnerable. Even his sons scolded him harshly, and when they did that, he would just pick up the *Naladiyar* and start reading.

Books and only books were his solace, his escape.

Maybe it was from books that he got the idea of feeding complete strangers.

Perimma was always worried about the house and added to that was her anxiety—how would their children get well-settled if her husband was so irresponsible? This constant worry and anxiety would reflect in her anger against the guests that Perippa brought home to be fed. Whenever she refused to feed them, Perippa would take that guest to Saraswathi Vilas nearby to feed them. Not a day passed without Perimma yelling at Perippa for feeding these good-for-nothing fellows. But he never changed.

Perippa had no bad habits; no *beedi*, no cigarette, no gambling. Sometimes he bought bananas and fed the temple cows. Once there was even a complaint that when he found a goat roaming on Vandikkaran Street he took it to a shop and bought some brinjal for the animal. What's more, one day—and Perimma shouted for all to hear—he bought some fish scraps from Muniyandi Vilas to feed two kittens roaming in the street. But that was Perippa. Though Perimma poured her bile on him all his life, he never blamed his wife, not even once.

Perimma however believed that he walked backwards because he was angry with her. Ever since he had started walking like that, she had lost her sleep. Some nights she kept the front door open and watched the street. They said that she also spoke in her sleep.

"The man is doing this only to punish me," she would complain to the women who were her neighbours.

It was difficult for people to comprehend why a man would do this to punish his wife.

Perippa was an impractical man and did not know how to live, this was Perimma's accusation. He worked in a store run by a co-operative society. Perimma always kept telling him that he should buy the wares sold at a low price from the store and sell them outside for a higher price. But Perippa was not willing to do that.

"The income you make is not enough for us to survive. Can't you stop this free hospitality?" Perimma scolded him.

"How does it matter which hungry stomach we feed?" Perippa asked.

"And to feed others, you will scrape my house out, is it? Don't you think you should save something for your children?"

"Who knows what tomorrow holds for us?"

"You want me to feed all and sundry, and then be driven to the street as a destitute?"

"We won't become poor if we feed one person."

"Let one more person enter this house to eat, and I will leave this house!" she screamed.

Perippa would then start reading the *Tiruvachagam* loud enough for her to hear. Perimma felt an intense helplessness and wailed with rage. Perippa would not speak to her for two days. Then one day again, suddenly, he would invite someone in to eat. This is how their life went on.

What had happened that made him start walking backwards was a mystery to everyone.

No one in our town could walk backwards like Perippa. Maybe in the whole world there are a few others like him. But I doubt they can walk as fast as he did.

It was the day that he and Perimma had to attend a wedding at Advocate Arunachalam's house. Perimma was certain that it was that very day when he started walking like that.

If we asked her what was unusual or special about that day, her answer was that it was the same daily drama, bringing a guest home for a meal. Because they were planning to attend the wedding, she had not done any cooking. Yet Perippa brought a mendicant, a *pandaram*.

"I can't serve food now, we have to go to the wedding," Perimma said.

"We will reach by the time they start serving food at the wedding. He has come walking all the way from Uppathur. Cook something for him." Perippa said.

The man too sat down promptly, ready to eat. Perimma was beside herself with rage, and poured a pot of water on that man. He stood up calmly, without a trace of anger.

"Blessed woman, be well," he said and walked away.

If the pandaram had reacted with anger, Perippa would have been quiet. But instead, he had given her a blessing.

"Are you a woman?" he yelled at Perimma.

Perimma could not control herself either, and she abused him terribly. He rushed out of the house and since that day, he started walking backwards.

Does bitterness make a man do this?

Perippa never shared his side of the story with anyone. But after that day, he neither brought home strangers to feed, nor did he eat at home. He had all his meals at a hotel. But he continued to live in that house.

What kind of a life was this? It puzzled everyone.

It was as if he was mocking the world by walking backwards. There were some who imitated his walking to ridicule him. He never got angry with them. He just went on walking as he wanted to.

What would change if we all walked backwards instead of walking straight ahead? I too tried to walk like Perippa. When I walked backwards, it seemed as if the whole earth had suddenly rolled over in its sleep. The vehicles, human activity, the trees on the roadside, everything changed. I learnt that forward motion and backward motion were not the same. It was difficult to walk with one's head turned around.

Perippa did not even turn his head to see the path he was walking on. He walked as if he had two additional eyes on the back of his head. No one ever saw him stumble or dash against anyone. Habit alone cannot achieve this. One needs a strong, firm and functioning mind to make this happen.

I asked Perippa why he walked so.

"To the man who walks backwards, the world is immense. We must not follow the world, we must make the world follow us," he replied.

I was too young then to understand what he meant and why he said that.

At that time, I often wondered if there was a bird that flew backwards like Perippa, or if there was an animal which moved like that. It was not just an oddity, it was a protest, an implacable stubbornness, a determined refusal to do as the world did.

After he began to walk backwards, Perippa also stopped travelling out of town. Home, work and temple—these were the only places that he went to. Perimma in fact considered this her triumph.

But Perippa's children kept criticising him all the time, especially my cousin Surendar Anna, who told him to his face that he was crazy and that he would achieve nothing by reading books. Perippa's other children, Shanti Akka and Divakar Anna, also fought with him and said that they found his mad behaviour offensive. Perippa did not say anything. He did not talk to anyone at home.

So what? Would ties break just because there was no conversation among the family?

I was really fond of Perippa. He would hold a newspaper in one hand and would swing his other hand as he walked backwards. He walked like that even when he had to cross the road. Muthusami Sir suggested that he keep a whistle to aid him at such times. But Perippa paid no heed to this advice.

When I was in college, I would go to the store where he worked because I wanted to walk with him. Even when he rose from his chair to fetch something from the shelves in the store, he walked backwards.

It amused people when he did that, and they laughed in front of him. Perippa too smiled. He worked hard and sincerely. He tended the store till eight at night, and returned home only after he had carefully noted down the day's accounts.

"Who are you angry with, Perippa?" I once asked him when I was walking with him.

"Why be angry? I am useless. When I am unable to feed a hungry person, what will I achieve by getting angry with anyone?"

"Then are you punishing yourself?"

"This is not punishment. This is freedom. When the whole world is going forward, I am the solitary walker going backwards. Am I not the one who is independent and free?"

"How is this freedom?"

"It can't be explained. It has to be lived."

I could never keep pace with Perippa. I would stop midway while he continued to walk home backwards.

Whenever I saw him, I thought this world is very strange. Every individual faces the world in his own way. It is easy to conform and take the beaten track, but it is a challenge to go against the stream.

Perimma kept hoping that eventually, some day, Perippa would change and become like everybody else. Even though there were no such indications, she clung on to that hope.

Then one day Perimma came home and began complaining loudly.

"Want to hear what this man is doing now? His mental condition has worsened. He stops while he is walking. And it would be fine if he stopped for five minutes when his legs hurt. But this man keeps standing in the same spot for hours! Two days ago, he stood in the same spot on Sekkalai Street from four o'clock in the evening to nine next morning. What shall I do with this lunatic? Why is this happening now?"

"What is this new confusion? Let me talk to him," Appa, my father, told her. I thought perhaps Perippa had really lost his mind. Then I wondered if he found happiness in standing as he did in walking backwards.

After the onset of this change, no one could predict when and where he would suddenly decide to stand still. He could not go to work, nor could he be entrusted to do anything. But he did not seem to care about all this.

When I heard that Perippa had been standing motionless for a day and a half under the neem tree near Panchupettai, I ran to see him. He kept standing there all day and all night...no food no sleep. It seemed as if he had turned into stone.

I went near him, held his hand and called him.

"Perippa!"

"It is blissful," he said. Then he opened his eyes and smiled at me.

I could not comprehend what was happening. This time Perimma did not leave him be. She had him lifted by two men who took him to a hospital in Madurai. They said it was schizophrenia. She brought him back after his treatment was over.

But even after he returned from the hospital, he continued to walk backwards. Only the swiftness that he had earlier was no longer there. It was then that something unexpected happened.

Perippa's eldest son, Surendar Anna, also began to walk backwards. He started going to work at the cement factory walking backwards just like Perippa—swiftly, without dashing against anyone. Perimma was unable to bear this. She cried, wailed, shouted and pleaded to god. But Surendar Anna paid no heed to his mother's emotions.

"Yenda, have you too lost your mind like that man? Why should you inherit your father's madness?"

"Don't criticise Appa. He is not an ordinary man. You won't understand."

When she heard this, her rage knew no bounds and she went to pick up a log of firewood to hit him. By then Surendar Anna had left the house.

Perimma just could not bear her son walking backwards like his father. She went to the temple and brought *vibhuti*, the sacred ash, and put it on his forehead. She consulted astrologers to find out about the movement of the planets in his horoscope. Often, she would curl up and lay down, and refuse to cook, saying she is unwell. Everyone said she behaved like a sick cat. Surendar Anna paid no heed to her.

The whole town was agog about the father and son who walked backwards. Perippa said nothing about his son's transformation.

One day I saw the two of them walking on the road. Surendar Anna could never catch up with Perippa and there was always a ten feet gap between them. Like two birds crossing each in the same sky, they went past each other, but never walked together side by side.

Surendar Anna laughed and said to me, "Family is a disease that affects a human being. The disease must be destroyed somehow."

I nodded, but I could not understand why they had transformed like this.

Suddenly one day, Perippa and Surendar Anna disappeared from town. No one could find out where they had gone or what had happened to them.

Perimma cursed that they will roam as beggars in front of some temple somewhere. But in the days that followed she never shut the door of their house. She started going to the cement factory to work. She began to talk to herself aloud, as though she was speaking to someone sitting near her. Sometimes she wailed loudly.

Twenty years after all this, once I came to hear that some *swami* was going to demonstrate walking on water in Kolkata, so I went to see. Arrangements had been made to feed everyone who came. The aroma of food wafted in the air all around. There was one swamiji with a thick beard and moustache, and everyone was falling at his feet to get his blessings. When I approached him, I saw who he was. It was Surendar Anna. He did not recognise me. He blessed me and gave me some *kumkum*.

"Swamiji, who is your guru?" someone asked him in Bengali.

"Mayilvahanam Swamigal."

Though his response was not clear, I knew at that instant that the name he uttered was my Perippa's name. The swamiji's eyes stared fixedly and vacantly into the distance just like Perippa's eyes. I did not reveal myself to him.

"Where is Mayilvahanam Swamigal?" the same devotee asked.

"He attained *jeeva samadhi*," the swamiji replied.

When I heard that, a gentle ache spread in my heart.

The swamiji was going to demonstrate walking on water before the crowd that evening. But I no longer had any desire to see that. When I returned home, I told my wife everything.

"Is your whole family like this?" she asked.

I was angry that she made fun of the matter like this. I wanted to tell Perimma the truth, and so I went to her place.

As a single parent, she had raised her daughter and her other son, got them married and now she had grandchildren too. Her face sagged with age, and she kept talking to herself.

Until I reached her house, I had the intention to tell her the truth. But when I saw her, I decided not to tell her anything. She began to speak about Perippa on her own.

"When we were leaving for the wedding at Advocate Arunachalam's place he brought the mendicant. In my anger I said, 'If you are a man, you must conduct yourself in a manner that would make you respectable, make people hold you in high regard and talk about you. This empty bravado is useless.' But it didn't provoke that man at all. He just laughed...a venomous laugh. From the next day, he started walking backwards...plain madness!"

I could not understand Perippa's mind at all. If he had begun to walk backwards only to punish Perimma, what kind of punishment was that? I felt I should talk to Appa about this. So I told him everything.

He said, "I don't know if he was a wise man or a fool. But one thing I understood clearly. A true human being is one who can feel another man's hunger. He never begged for food from anyone. But he also never said an ill word about families that did not feed the hungry. The simplest way to punish another is to punish oneself, isn't it? He did only what he liked; he did not change himself for anyone. It is tough to live like that. He had no grudge against the world that mocked him. You and I are ordinary persons. But he was not like that. To those who understood him, he was a *gnani*. To the rest he was a good-for-nothing."

I was confused.

"So can a man walk on water?"

"Even an insect can walk on water, that is no big deal. It is not necessary for a man to be wise to walk on water. If the mind and body are aligned with one another, you can do anything. We must keep them under control. My anna had that control."

Perippa's face came to my mind's eye. Appa must have been thinking of him too. He spoke with regret in his voice.

"If the world does not understand a person, it is fine. But if his own family does not, then that life is hell. Neither the world nor his own understood my brother. Yet he did not think it was a big loss. Tell me, how many are like that?"

When I heard this, I realised I would never see Perippa again, and a feeling of sadness came and sat heavily on my heart.

Fire Never Forgets

"There is no such thing as the present. It is an outright lie. We are forever thinking of the future, and it is the future which reveals itself as the present. It is the thought that we are thirsty that makes us stretch our hand towards the water pot. There is only the past and the future. There is no such thing as the present, no such thing."

The words of the islander filled me with surprise. I recorded it on my tape-recorder.

In the last few years, I have been engaged in the research and study of rare tribes and their world. My research is on those who live in isolation in caves and valleys, untouched by the transformation that scientific inventions and modern amenities have brought about. For my study I have travelled to various parts of India and studied different tribes.

Many of them were still under the impression that the world was somewhere far away. Some raised their hand towards the sky to indicate the world. Some women touched their bellies to show where the world is, while others said that it was, in fact, their mind that formed the world.

The tribespeople mocked me when I told them about the world as I knew it. A tribe in Odisha firmly believed that the world was just a figment of imagination. After I started my study, I too have begun to wonder if the world really just existed in our imagination.

It was my plan for a long time to visit Obu Island situated in the Indian Ocean. No more than seventy-eight persons were allowed to live on that island. This bar on population was imposed because Obu was next to Muyal Island, where a centre of the National Institute of Oceanography was situated. Anyone who went to Obu without proper permission would be punished with imprisonment.

The residents of Obu were however unaware of all this. All they knew was that motorboats went to and fro across the sea around Muyal Island, which they saw from Obu some distance away.

Obu Island was an old island which had many coral reefs. The tribespeople who lived there fished only using traditional methods, that is, by spearing the fish. They never caught even one fish more than what they needed for food. Further, their immunity against diseases was very high, so they never fell sick. I had heard that their life expectancy was over hundred and twenty years. These facts had been noted by Dr Immanuel who was engaged in research during the British period. After him no one had visited Obu. It remained a forbidden island for many years.

I waited in Delhi for three weeks for the Union Government to grant me permission. They allowed me only because I was doing my research from a university in the USA. But I was granted only two days for the visit.

There were no transport facilities to Obu available. One had to hire a motorboat to reach the island. So I hired a boat for a day from Joshua Martin. The boatman, Mathias, was from Semparai Island. He was grey-haired and his thick lips were chapped and swollen. His attention was focused only on steering the boat, he did not respond to any of my questions.

When we crossed Muyal Island, the security guards stopped the boat to inspect us. They asked for the Government permit, checked it and let me go, warning that I must return in two days. I nodded.

"What are you doing here in Muyal Island? What research?" I asked.

"Study of marine algae."

Why did they need so much security for the study of marine algae? Why did they need metal fences ringing the island?

Without further questions, I proceeded towards Obu. The waves were not very fierce. Terns circled over the blue sea, and the sky seemed to lose some of its blue in contrast.

As the boat moved along, the sea changed colour. After a point, it turned from blue to black. The waves too quietened. As the boat plowed on, the sea turned darker. It was puzzling, the water's blackness. Sunlight shimmered on the waves like a film of oil. Wherever we see it, whenever we see it, the sea never ceases to inspire wonder in us. It remains a deep mystery. The boat moved towards Obu in the gentle wind.

I was surprised when I set foot on the island. There were no houses—just one cave, a huge cave. The islanders lived, slept, ate and did everything in that cave. The Obu people were all over six feet tall, and the women were taller than the men. They were dressed in clothing made of rush.

I asked Mathias to be with me so I could communicate with the Obu folk. Yet, they did not understand my questions and some even laughed at them.

I could not fathom why they laughed when I asked them what, according to them, was the world. I asked Mathias why they were amused. He too laughed.

Only two of the Obu people were permitted to be in touch with the rest of the world. They could cross the sea and go to far-off towns and it was through them that some help could be secured.

They said that Pandimadevi, the island deity, decided who should connect with the outside world.

I asked Mathias to find out how these individuals were chosen. No one replied at first. Then one woman answered boldly.

"The one who receives the dream is chosen to connect with the outside world."

When I countered that anyone could dream, she shook her head in disagreement. "Those who can have no contact with the outside world never dream. Dreaming is dangerous. The gods will not permit it," she said.

I met one of the men who had been chosen to travel outside the island and spoke to him.

"We don't need the outside world. We are a world by ourselves, a separate world."

"Do you have a mythological story? Why are you scared of the outside?"

"There is one story. Panna knows it."

They took me to an old man who was more than a hundred years old. His hair was white like the stork's down, his brows thick, his skin dry and wrinkled, and his nails uncut and long.

"Who are you?" Panna asked me softly.

"I am doing research on the islanders."

"Why do you want to study us?"

"So that the world gets to know about you."

"Why should the world get to know us?"

I had no answer.

"So that you may contact the world," I said, although it was not an answer to his question.

"We do not need the world. We have come away from it."

"How long have you been living on this island? Don't you wish to leave this place and move away?"

"We are barred from crossing the sea. So we have sought sanctuary on this island. A woman's curse keeps chasing us."

"Whose curse? What curse? Please tell me the story."

"A woman who was denied justice ordered the fire against us. Even now the fire keeps chasing us. So we don't use fire—it has eyes, the eyes will identify us."

"You don't use fire at all? Never?"

"We don't, never have. We have stayed away from fire for several generations. And you know what, our women do not let their babies suckle on their left teat. That belongs to god."

"Who is the woman? And why did she put this curse?"

"It is a long story that lives in our memory. It all happened more than a thousand years ago. Then we lived in a city, a big city. It had four concentric ramparts. We lived inside the second rampart. A river flowed outside the fortress. Storks with greenish legs and soft wings stood on the banks waiting to catch the fish that swam against the current.

"On the lanes that ran as wide as the river, broad-shouldered and well-built men roamed about, happily drinking *kallu,* shooing away the bees that swarmed around the drink.

"Women with shoulders as slender as bamboo and white conch bangles on their slim wrists worshipped the god with grains and flowers.

"The servants who worked in the mansions ground fragrant things like sandalwood and musk on grinding-stones the colour of horse gram.

"The entrance to the palace looked like it was carved out of a mountain, and it was large enough to allow elephants returning triumphantly from the battlefield to walk through it with the flags on their backs aloft. The courtyard spread wide, and the king would come out at night to savour the moonlight that shone there. There was a fountain with a spout shaped like a shark from whose mouth water burbled out.

"Greek lamps carved like maidens were filled with oil and thick wicks were lit up to chase away the darkness indoors. The guests who visited our homes would be served succulent cuts of roasted mutton with fragrant fine rice like thin buds. Places were set up for feeding the poor and the helpless. White rice and *oon soru,* a meat and rice dish, would be distributed.

"Once a merchant from Puhar came to our city with his wife. He was arrested on suspicion of stealing and was executed without a trial. When the young wife came to know, she was enraged. She came to the palace of the Pandya king and begged for justice. When the king learnt the truth, he admitted his error. But her rage was not quenched. She twisted and tore her left breast and threw it, and from it rose a fire that set the city aflame. The king, filled with remorse, gave up his life.

"The king's sister Pandimadevi took his lifeless body and with a hundred faithful followers left the city. The fire chased them as they went. We are the descendants of those hundred.

"To escape the fire sent by the *pathni deivam*, the woman goddess, Pandimadevi entered the sea. The fire kept searching for her with the help of the wind. She travelled in a boat with the dead king's body for a long time and reached this island of Obu. She hid herself in this cave. This is where the king was buried.

"We are people who were driven away. We are people who lost our land. So we do not get dreams. We do not use fire because we are afraid it will recognise us. We now wait for the one-breasted woman's anger to cool down.

"Every year on the night of Chitra Pournami, we take the Pandya king's sword that Pandimadevi had brought with her and let it afloat on the sea. When the anger of Kotravai, the goddess, cools down, the sword will become a flower. We believe that only when the flower blooms in the sea, we can leave this island and go. The sword has not changed yet, the flower has never bloomed. We have been waiting for generations."

As I listened to their tale, my wonder grew. I interrupted the narration and said, "This is only a story. It did not happen in reality. What you narrated is the story of *Silappadikaram*, the epic written by Ilango."

"For you it is a tale, but for us it is the truth, it is our life," Panna replied.

"Even if it is true, that Madurai no longer exists. There is nothing remaining of the fire set by Kannagi. Your fear is futile. Time has erased the identity of Kannagi and there is not a single temple dedicated to her in Tamil Nadu."

"That is a lie! No one can forget Kannagi. She is the one who demands justice. She appears when injustice prevails. She will not forgive our wrongdoing. Fire never forgets."

"I don't know how to make you believe me. How can anyone remain angry for a thousand years? Can't you see it is a folly to believe that?"

"Has not fire remained fire from times immemorial? Doesn't it burn us when we touch it? Is there anything such as old fire and new fire? Who knows how many years must pass before a sin can be forgiven? Don't you know that for some wrongs there is no forgiveness? Generations may pass...but there is no forgiveness."

"With the passage of time anything can be forgiven."

"It is not so easy. The anger of men will subside, but not divine wrath. Injustice is never forgiven. The justice that was denied will for generations remain in the wounded hearts, it will take root there and grow."

"But you did not do any wrong. How can the people be punished for what the king did?"

"We are loyal to him, we have eaten his salt. The shadow of his sin thus falls on us."

"This is ignorance, a foolish belief!" I said aloud.

"Beliefs must not be shattered."

I kept trying to make him understand but he refused to be convinced. I asked him if he had anything that Pandimadevi brought with her to the island. He said he had a box made of palm leaf, an *olai petti.*

The box was kept under the seat dedicated to Pandimadevi. He opened it for my sake. There was a broken bit of a *silambu*, an anklet.

It was incredible. That was Kannagi's silambu, the silambu she had flung before the Pandya king!

I eagerly wanted to touch it and asked him if I could.

"It is forbidden." His voice was strained.

"How long are you going to wait like this?"

"Till the flower blooms in the sea," he said calmly.

I felt a deep sadness within me when I heard this.

On one side there is state-of-the-art technology, extraordinary inventions of science, buildings reaching out to the skies and myriad luxuries, and on the other side, in some corner, there lies an island where people still live in fear of the fire.

Will the sins of the past keep chasing the present?

As that islander had said, is the present a lie?

Can forgiveness erase injustice?

Will the victims of murder wait eternally for justice?

How many years will the unrelenting fury last?

These were questions that had no answers and I was...puzzled, perplexed and confused.

A Beast Called Home

"Appa, it seems you used to write poems," said Priya, tall and curly haired, in tenth class now.

Madan was dyeing his moustache, standing in front of the mirror.

"Who told you?" He was surprised.

"Aachi told me. Appa, write a poem for me. I want to give one to Kevin for his birthday."

Dipping the brush in the dye and carefully applying the colour on his sideburns, he replied, "I don't know, my dear."

"Amma also says she doesn't know...now whom will I ask?"

He noticed a black spot of dye on his ear and carefully wiped it.

"What kind of poem do you want?"

"Something about friendship...ten lines would be enough."

"Why don't you just copy one from some book and give it?"

"It is Kevin's birthday, Appa. I want it to be *my* poem, an original one."

"Then you write."

"But I can't think of anything to write...and there isn't a single book of poems in our house."

"Who would read poetry?"

"Aachi said that you used to read poetry a lot, that you used to borrow books from the library and read."

"That was during my school days. Later I stopped."

"Why, Pa?"

"Didn't like to..."

"Kevin writes excellent poems in English, Pa. He even gave me one for my birthday...didn't you read it too?"

He nodded, indicating that he had.

"Kevin's birthday is on Sunday. By then please write a poem somehow...please, Appa!"

"Let me see." He went out to the balcony and stood in the sun.

Times have changed.

My daughter asks me for a poem to gift her classmate Kevin on his birthday, Madan thought. Kevin comes over without any fear or hesitation to their house to chat with Priya. Some days the two of them go out to the shopping mall together to eat and watch movies, and the sound of them talking over the phone can be heard late into the night.

Priya also goes to Kevin's house. Kevin's mother even brought a birthday gift for Priya. What a transformation in thirty years! In his days, parents were not like this, nor was he like Kevin. But he too liked a girl, she was also a Priya. She was his schoolmate. It was for her that he wrote poems.

In a small town like the one he grew up in, standing on the street chatting with a girl or going to watch a film together was unthinkable, especially if one was still in school. Any grownup would reprimand a schoolboy if he was seen talking to a schoolgirl.

Time has not only brought with it modern gadgets of communication, but also a better understanding and a broader outlook of relationships. Or does it seem to be so only on the surface?

Boys and girls at age sixteen have always been the same. But now the iron wall that restrained them and kept them separate has been broken. It is no longer considered wrong if they go out to eat or watch a movie together. But still, this is not accepted in all homes. Many parents continue to look at their children with suspicion and keep them under surveillance. They find faults and reprimand their children. And in the process, one of the parents, either the mother or the father, usually becomes an enemy.

This is not love. It is not necessary to ask her if she is in love with Kevin, Madan reflected.

"Don't be stupid. I want to study further, and this is just friendship." Priya's reply would come in a flash.

Why was this friendship not permitted in the past? Why was it impossible to be friends with a girl without having to be in love with her? Madan had learnt from his father much of what one should not do. And he was quite shocked to realise that on many occasions he was unconsciously behaving just like his father. "Appa" is not an individual, "Appa" is a kind of behaviour, an attitude, and Madan was very careful to never become as short-tempered as Appa. He did not want to treat his children the way his father treated him.

In particular, he wanted to be careful and ensure that their home was not a place that was loathed by his children. Thankfully Rama too did not behave like his Amma. Madan's wife understood the changes her children were going through and could handle their confusion very well.

As he was leaving for work, he decided that he must compose a poem for Priya. But it was not as easy as he thought. He could not write more than one or two words. How many poems had he written when he was young? Why did he plug the spring of poetry? It was Appa's anger that had driven him away from this art.

After a lengthy struggle, he could finish writing ten lines. But it could not be called poetry, he thought. He tore it up and stared out of his office window into the distance.

It is not possible to recapture the past when it has already slipped through the fingers. But the memory was still fresh and green in his heart. As if it was just yesterday that he had gone to school in his khaki trousers and white shirt. It seemed that the incidents in his past had happened to someone else.

At that time they lived in a small town called Aruppukottai. Madan did not have a room of his own in the rented house where they lived. In all those years, Appa did not build a house that they could call their own. They always lived in rentals. Madan, his mother and his two younger sisters slept in a single room. It comprised a tiny hall, a tiny kitchen and a tiny storeroom in which they kept their cupboard and all their provisions. They used the room to change clothes.

Till he was in the tenth standard, Madan had not given any thought to the house. But when he came to the eleventh, he underwent many changes. He looked at himself frequently in the mirror. He stroked the thin moustache that had recently sprouted and squeezed out the pimples. And he often wondered why they lived in that house and why Appa could not find a bigger house. He asked Amma one day.

"Big house means the rent will be high. Who will pay that? When you start earning, you can find yourself a big house."

"So until then we have to live in this rat-hole?"

"What can *I* do? You ask your Appa."

How could he talk to Appa? He would shout at the slightest excuse, for anything and everything. Amma had asked him many times to build a house. He had the same reply.

"If they transfer me to another location, we would have to move. So tell me, in which town should I build the house?"

Appa was a government servant. It is true that he was often transferred, but it was always within the district. For the last six years the family lived in the same town. Appa alone went to the new location of work.

When he turned sixteen, Madan felt embarrassed to sleep in the same room with the others. How nice it would be if he had a room of his own! A room where he could sleep as he pleased, read when he wanted to...at least if there was a terrace that would be enough. But the house had no place for privacy.

That is why he started to go to his friend Anand's house. There was a separate room on the first floor which you could go straight up to after entering through the gate. He had stayed many nights there, in Anand's room, when they returned from late night shows at the movie theatre.

It was then that Madan had started writing poems. To tell the truth, the reason he started writing poems was Priya. It was for her that he wrote. But in those days, he did not have the guts to read them out or give them to her. He kept writing poems in a small notebook which had a picture of Saraswathi on its cover. In it, he had covered one whole page with their names: 'Priya ♡ Madan', scribbled over and over again. One day he tried to draw a sketch of her. But try as he might, the sketch did not look like her.

Priya's house was on Subbiah Pillai Street. Every morning while cycling on his way to school, he would stop in that street.

Did she have a separate room in her house for herself? Where did she sleep? Where did she study? On which plate did she eat? Thoughts about her would keep swirling in Madan's head as he stood there in front of her house.

Priya came out of her house only at eight-thirty. The girls' school where she studied was nearby. If you walked fast, you could reach the school in five minutes. Madan would follow her on his cycle. She was aware of this, and she walked with a smile, her head bent.

Inhibition and shyness stopped him from approaching her. In the evening, after school, he sat with Anand in the playground and just talked about Priya. Anand's brother and Priya's brother were friends as both played hockey. So Anand had gone over to Priya's house a few times. Madan felt happy when Anand talked about that.

After tenth class, Madan changed schools. He chose to study science just because Priya had opted for that. It was then that he came to know of the Gopalan Reading Room. It operated from someone's house. Gopalan offered free tuition there. Anyone could borrow books from his library, and there were many books on communism. Gopalan never went out as his legs were polio-afflicted. One reason why Madan visited the library was because Priya often went there to borrow books.

It was when he began going there for tuition classes that he found out the many poetry books there. One day he picked one and brought it a home. It was easy to read, and as he read, he was filled with joy and it awoke something in him. He wondered how mere words could give so much happiness. He wrote some poems similar to the ones in the book.

Madan showed his poems to Gopalan.

"Did you really write this?" Gopalan was doubtful.

He nodded in assent.

"It is very good. Write a lot. We can send it to *Thamarai*." He said encouragingly, and then suggested some books to Madan.

Thereafter he was always seen with a book of poetry in his hand.

One day Priya came on her cycle to borrow a book. When she had gone in, he placed a sheet with one of his poems inside a copy of the *Malaimathi* magazine and kept it on her cycle carrier. When Priya returned, she noticed the *Malaimathi*. She turned around to see who had done it. Then with a smile she left.

Next day when he went to the reading room, the magazine was there. The paper on which he had written the poem was also there, but there was something new. On the reverse, Priya had written a poem.

Madan was surprised. Did girls write poems? It was a love poem, just four lines. The joy it gave him was immeasurable, and he read it again and again.

She liked his poem. She wrote poems too. So she too must read a lot of poetry. He forgot his studies and drowned himself in love poems. He wrote countless poems.

The poems had to be kept hidden somewhere and that was a problem. If he kept them in the cupboard someone might find and read them. So he hid them in an old pillow which he kept in the storeroom.

One evening he returned home to see his father sitting on the cane chair, looking furious. Beside him was the poetry notebook and some sheets. Madan burst out in anger.

"Who asked you to take these?"

"Is this the shit that you study?"

"You know zilch about poems! This is personal to me."

"What personal? I pay for your studies, not for you to write poems. A good-for-nothing fellow like you will end up begging on the streets."

"Let me beg...Give me back my notebook now."

"I want to frame each of these poems and hang them on these walls. Let these be with me."

"Do as I say and return the book."

"Who the hell is Priya? Who is this bitch? You are writing for her, aren't you?" He began tearing up the sheets.

"Appa, listen to me...Give it back!" Madan shouted.

"What did you say? How dare you scowl at me?"

"Don't do that, Appa. Listen to me, give it back."

"Ey, go throw it in that stove, burn it. Only then will this dog change his ways," he said to his wife.

"Amma, if you just touch it...that's it...I will hang myself! I will!"

"Get lost! Hang yourself. Who is holding you back?"

"Ey, don't be brainless, you...I want my poetry book back."

"What...you *naayi*! Exceeding your limits, aren't you?" Appa leapt up to hit him, but he dodged. Appa lost his balance and almost fell. Amma screamed.

By then Appa's rage was uncontrollable. As he came at him again, Madan grabbed his father's shoulders and shoved him back. He fell backwards with a big thud.

"Ayyo! Ayyo!" Appa started yelling.

Amma, by then in tears, was scolding Madan.

"What is this? You think you can hit your father?"

"I didn't hit him at all. He fell down on his own."

"A son who hits his father will be doomed."

"Who hit him? You are talking like a crazy person!"

"Yes, *da, I* am crazy...and you are a genius!" she yelled back.

"I can't explain or make you understand anything," Madan shouted as he bent down to pick up the scattered sheets.

"You step inside this house once more, naayi, and I'll break your leg!" Appa went on shouting.

Why is my home like this? Why does Appa behave so badly? Can't I even keep my poems to myself, away from their prying eyes? Madan thought. He picked up the notebook and went to see Anand. Anand was not at home; he and his brother had gone to the railway station.

So Madan walked to the station. As he walked in the dark, he felt like hanging himself. Anand was waiting there to see someone off. When he saw Madan, he came up to him.

"What, da?"

"I want to speak with you," Madan replied.

"Let the train leave. You sit there and wait," he pointed towards a cement bench. Madan chose a spot where the light was dim.

Until the train arrived, Madan's fingers softly stroked Priya's poems.

After his brother boarded the train, Anand came to him and asked, "What happened, da?"

"Problem at home, da. Appa tore up all the poems I had written."

"Let it go. We can write some more."

"I hate being at home."

"Where will you go?"

"I want to die."

"Why do you speak like this? Let's go to my place...come."

"I will not go back to that house."

"We will decide that later."

"They say all kinds of nonsense about Priya, da."

"Why did you keep all those poems at home?"

"Where else would I keep them? There is only one room."

"You could have given them to me to keep, no?"

Madan was silent.

"Shall we go?" Anand asked him.

"I won't. You go."

"Why do you talk to this? Come, we will go watch some movie."

"That fellow came to beat me, da."

"Don't keep thinking about it. Let's eat something and go."

"No, da. I want to die."

"You come now," Anand said firmly as he pulled him.

The two of them went to a parotta shop. Madan's mouth felt bitter as if he had jaundice. *Ninaithale Inikkum* was being screened at Saraswathi Theatre. It had been playing for fifty days, so there was not much of a crowd for the night show.

Madan just could not focus on the movie. What should he do? Continue with school? Or drop out? Should he tell Priya about this? How would he face Appa again?

The same thoughts played in his mind again and again, even after the show was over and he had returned to Anand's.

Appa was an educated man—why did he loathe poetry so? Had he never fallen in love? Ever?

He did not sleep a wink that night.

In the morning his mother came to Anand's house. She was narrating everything that had happened to Anand's mother. Anand's mother too joined her in scolding Madan.

"Why spend time on this poetry and such trash when you have to study? Just finish your studies and get a job."

Madan did not say anything.

"Go to school like a good boy and focus on your studies," Amma said, frowning at him.

"I am not going to study at all."

"We will discuss that after we go home. Let's go." Amma pulled him by his hand.

"I won't," Madan said stubbornly.

"If you don't come, I won't go." Amma started sobbing.

Chey...why are these people torturing me? He thought as he walked back home with his mother. He felt as if the house was scoffing at him as he approached it.

Appa was leaving for office.

"Enough of that reading room and that library. Come home straight from school from now on. You must study properly."

Madan did not even look at him.

"All night Amma was crying. She even kept the front door open," Madan's sister said with disapproval.

Irritated, Madan went to the bathroom. How he wished he could become ten years older in a single day! How many more days would he have to remain caged in this house?

He got ready to go to school and was about to leave when Amma stuck five rupees in his hand.

"That Priya says she does not even know who you are...then why do you follow her all the time? If you don't study, what will you do? How will you survive?"

"Did you go to Priya's house, Amma?"

"Yes, I did."

"Who asked you to go there? Why, Ma? Why do all of you together want to take my life?"

"Why, what is wrong if I go there?"

"You are mad! What did you say to them?"

"I told them that my son will not follow her anymore."

"Ayyo, who followed her, Ma?"

"Didn't you fill the whole book with her name 'Priya'?"

"So...?"

"Dear god! Your father said you can go to hell...but I can't say that too, can I? That is why I went to her house and told them."

"I am not going to study. I won't go to school."

"Then go die."

"You think I won't?"

"Why should *you* die, da? *I* will die and then you and your father can punch each other as much as you want." Amma started to beat her breast and wail.

Madan picked up his bag and set off for school.

He resolved to never write poems again. He would ask Anand to burn all the poems that were with him.

He took a different route to go to school, one that did not pass by Priya's house.

When he returned home from school that evening, all his anger towards his father transformed into anger against the house. Home was a beast that was trying to grasp him in its jaws, its fangs long and sharp. He must not become its prey. He flung a stone at the house. It hit the wall and fell down.

He left his school bag inside and came out, but realised that he could no longer go to Anand's house either, it was too embarrassing. In a single day all the exit passages had been barred. This house was the only refuge for him.

Madan sat on the floor and pretended to study with his book open in front of him.

Appa came in. He brought a bag of *pakoda*s and sweet *boondi.* He took out the boondi and asked Madan to have some. It was as if the events of yesterday had not happened at all.

Madan's throat closed up. He could not swallow the sweet.

On his way home from office, Madan entered a bookstore. It had been many years since he had last gone to buy a book. He did not know what to buy. He could not find any of the books that he had read when he was sixteen. After a long search, he bought four books of poetry.

"Are they poetry books, Appa?" A surprised Priya asked when he reached home.

"Yes...Mustn't I write a poem for you?"

"I wrote one by myself." She smiled.

"How?" He was surprised.

"It was Amma who helped. Amma recites poetry so beautifully... haven't you ever heard her recite, Appa?"

He had no idea that Rama liked poetry or that she could recite poems.

"Show it to me."

Priya stretched out a hand holding a sheet.

The poem was excellent.

"Do you really write poems?" He asked Rama, surprised.

"Used to. They would be published in our college magazine."

"You have never told me."

"Because you never asked!" Rama laughed.

Why was it so entrenched in his mind that poetry was only for men?

"Why did you stop writing poems?" He asked Rama.

"That's a story!" She laughed.

Madan did not ask her to tell him the story, nor did she tell him willingly. But both their eyes filled with tears.

Sitridazh

When we knocked on the door, we did not expect to hear the voice that answered—a gruff voice called out, "Some rascal is at the door. Go, open and see."

We stood hesitantly outside. It must have been three in the afternoon, and the street was deserted. It was a narrow street along the post office.

In a few minutes, an elderly lady wearing a green checkered saree slowly walked to the door. It squeaked as she opened it.

She glared at us.

"Whom do you want?"

When we said we wanted to see Narasimhan Sir, she scowled.

"Go to the back." She pointed towards the back end of the house. The three of us moved cautiously in that direction.

In the hall, there was a cane chair with a heap of dirty clothes on it. A pair of black pants hung from a nail on the wall. A man lay on a mat spread out on the floor. He wore a purple lungi, but no shirt. His heavy paunch was very hairy, his jowls drooping. He glared at us with red eyes.

In a room inside, a TV was on. A woman sat on a cot watching TV and folding washed laundry. All the walls were dull brown. None of the windows were open. There was one calendar with a picture of Saibaba on the wall.

It was an old house, long and narrow, with the rooms arranged in a line. In the rear to the north there was a small room. A torn old saree was hung as a screen at its entrance. When we pulled it aside, we saw Narasimhan sleeping on a steel cot. Perspiration ran down his back. One leg stuck out of the cot—he was a tall man, and the cot was not long enough for him. His arms looked thin. He was wearing a *khadar* undershirt and a coloured dhoti. There was one very tiny window in the room. There was a table fan on a wooden stool, but it was not on. I stood wondering whether to wake him up. Mohan gestured that we should leave. But Tirugnanam moved closer to Narasimhan and touched his shoulder gently.

"Ayya...Sir..." He called softly.

Narasimhan must have been in a deep sleep; this did not wake him up.

I looked around the room. There was a small clay pot and a metal box under the cot. On a small wooden stool near the cot lay a half-eaten apple. Flies hovered around the fruit. There were medicines: many kinds of tablets and a jar of *churanam*. On a drooping clothesline hung two khadar towels.

Taped to the wall was a picture of the German poet Rilke that had been torn out of some book. A young Rainer Maria Rilke. It seemed as if he was gazing at the strange atmosphere of the room.

By fifty years of age, Narasimhan had published three collections of poems, a collection of translated poetry, and two collections of articles and essays on poetry. His poems were translated into English and French. He had not received any award till date. There were no book launches or readings for his books. His books did not carry his photograph nor even a small note about him. As far as one could recollect, he had never been invited to literary functions. But serious readers of literature loved his poetry and frequently referred to his poems.

In the last fifteen years, the literary scene has completely transformed and a new generation of readers has come up who are neither aware of Narasimhan nor of his great poetry. No one even knew that he was still alive.

We remembered Narasimhan when we read his poems which were re-published in the poetry journal *Mudivili*. Tirugnanam was surprised to learn that Narasimhan lived in their very town. It was he who suggested that we should ask him for a poem and that is why we were there.

"Let him sleep. We should leave," I said softly.

Tirugnanam obviously did not agree.

"Ayya!" He called in a loud voice.

Startled awake, Narasimhan turned over. He was surprised to see three strange young men in his room. He rubbed his eyes, and leaning on his elbows tried to raise himself up. He was so thin that his rib cage stuck out. The man had lost a lot of weight. Some thin grey hair remained on the back of his head. He groped for his spectacles, found the pair and wore them. Then he sat leaning on the pillow.

"Have you been waiting for a long time?"

"We came just now. You were asleep," Mohan replied.

"The heat is too much, I couldn't bear it. I was reading Kabir and had dozed off." He picked up the small English book that was near his pillow, and showed it to us.

The room smelt of something like pesticide.

"There are no chairs here. Please sit on the floor. Move the fan to the side," he said.

The three of us sat near the cot.

"We are publishing a small literary magazine called 'Agavulagu'. We have come to ask you for a poem," Tirugnanam spoke.

"Are you all college students?"

"I own a fruit store, he studied engineering but did not complete his studies, and Mohan runs a tuition centre." It was Tirugnanam again.

"Do all three of you write?"

"Two of us write poetry, he only translates. For our last issue he translated William Carlos Williams." He pointed to me.

"Good poet. I have read him too," Narasimhan said. Then he was lost in thought.

The room was too stuffy and perspiration ran down my neck.

"What did you say is your journal's name?"

"Agavulagu," replied Tirugnanam.

"The Inner World—it's a nice name. How many issues have come out till now?"

"Three, and the fourth is in the making. That is why we have come to you with the request."

"It has been twenty years since I stopped writing poems. Many new poets like you have come up...Why do you still need us?"

"It's not like that, Ayya. We love your poems. You had titled your collection of poems 'Sodium'. What a superb title! That too fifty years ago! You have written so many experimental poems which are the guiding stars for today's poets."

"I was a student of chemistry, so it is natural that my poems would smell of chemicals!" Narasimhan smiled faintly.

"None of your books are available in print any longer. They should be printed again now, no?" Mohan asked.

"Who will read them? When they came out years ago, even then, only a hundred copies were sold. Tamil culture has a heritage of two thousand years of poetry, but you cannot sell two thousand copies of a Tamil poet's book. That is the reality."

"Even today poems don't sell," said Tirugnanam.

We heard footsteps approaching the room. Narasimhan's face changed.

The man who had been lying in the hall had got up. He shouted, "Who parked the bike close to the wall of the house opposite? Move it right away, they are complaining."

Mohan rose.

That man glared at him and then turned back. After he had disappeared from sight, Narasimhan asked in a quavering voice.

"Did they abuse you when you came in?"

Tirugnanam remained silent.

"No one in this house likes me," he continued. "I can't describe the intensity of their hatred. Even if someone is here just to visit me, they will spew venom at them. This one, who went back just now, is my eldest son. The woman inside is his wife. No one likes me. You know why? They don't want me to read or write. They say I have ruined myself by reading books, they think I am half-mad. I still receive my pension, and they spend it all. What kind of creatures...I have given up, they are beyond redemption. Living a life surrounded by hatred is living in hell. The hell Dante had written about is nothing compared to this. Yet I have got used to this hell."

"Even my father doesn't like the idea of reading books," Tirugnanam said.

Narasimhan nodded.

"Every family is like that. If you start reading, you will start thinking independently, and then you won't listen to them. That is what they fear. A family will accept a drunkard but not a poet. This is our culture." His voice expressed intense anger and regret.

Mohan came back after having moved his bike away.

As he was about to sit down, Narasimhan asked him for some water from the pot. Mohan dipped the glass inside the pot, but there was no water.

"Shall I ask them?" Tirugnanam came forward.

"No one will bring you water. Just go to the kitchen and get some water from the tap."

Tirugnanam carried the pot to the kitchen.

Narasimhan sat thinking, his head bent.

"One should not live long. If we do, we have to suffer all kinds of indignities. Two years ago, I slipped and fell in the bathroom and broke my hip bone. I was in the hospital for three months. When

I returned home after recovery, there was not a single book left in the house. They had sold everything to the waste-paper man. It was unbearable for me, I wept. My son asks me what I would achieve by reading at my age. Tell me, is there an age for reading? I can only bang my head for having this idiot of a son. And not just books, the notebooks in which I had written my poems, my old diaries... everything had been thrown out. I already know what will happen after I die. Fortunately, I had kept four books in the box containing my old dhotis. Those are the only books that remain. And I keep reading them again and again. I became a corpse when my books left me, nothing but a corpse...and only corpses don't read books."

He paused as tears streamed down his eyes. He wiped them away with the back of his hand.

"You are my grandson's age. I shall give you a grandfatherly advice: enough of reading and writing. If you give these up, at least you will live happily."

"This is the same thing we hear at home." Mohan sounded irritated, "But I will not change myself for anyone."

Narasimhan stared at him. Then nodding in assent, he said, "Even I am like you. What I said, I said out of frustration. Enough about me. Tell me about yourself. How much of your own money have you spent in publishing this journal?"

"A little more than twenty thousand," Tirugnanam said.

"I have never gone out to meet any writer, like you are doing now. Maybe it was inhibition, maybe it was fear. I thought, why should a poet need friends? Even if a reader praised my poems, I would feel shy. It seemed like someone was watching me bathe naked."

"The custom of feeling shy when praised went out of the window with other traditions of your times," Mohan said.

Narasimhan then turned to look at me.

"This young man hasn't spoken a word since you came. Do translators not speak?"

"I don't know what to say."

"I too was like that. And look at me babbling now, all because of what this house did to me."

"Why are you in this house of hatred? Why don't you go and live alone somewhere?" Mohan asked.

"Fear. The fear of being alone. Isn't that why I married? Instead of severing myself from fear, I had been nurturing it. Even now the fear has not gone."

"Is it the fear of death?"

"No, Appa. It is the fear of not knowing how to live. Sodium, you see, if it mixes with water, there will be fire. That is its nature. I am like that. I can't mix even with water."

"Do you think maybe your family would have accepted you if you had attained fame as a poet?" Mohan asked.

"The problem was not money or fame. They can't accept that I have a world of my own and my own aesthetic taste. Instead of that, if I too like any other person watched TV serials, gossiped with others, or had been jealous of the next man, the family would have accepted me. Rilke says that most of our experiences cannot be expressed and they happen in a space where no word has entered. I completely relate to it. This body that is Narasimhan is eighty-two years old, but the poet in me is older than two thousand years. I live in words, I hide myself in words. Each word is a cave. And that is where I am hiding."

Tirugnanam looked at him with wonder as suddenly Narasimhan seemed transformed. His wife called out in a loud voice as she went to the kitchen, "Enough of idle chatter. You may leave."

Like the glow of a lamp that is blown out suddenly, Narasimhan's words died. We felt as though darkness had enveloped us.

"Ayya, we will leave," Mohan said. Tirugnanam took some water and drank as he tried to hide his disappointment.

"Can you do me a favour?" Narasimhan asked in a weak voice.

"Of course, Ayya."

"It has been years since I stepped out of the house. Now I just walk indoors with a walking stick. Will you take me to the end of the road and bring me back?"

"Let us go, Ayya."

"I hope it is no trouble?"

"Let us go to the shop at the end of the road and have tea, Ayya," Mohan said.

Narasimhan got up. Only now we could see how tall he was—more than six feet. He grabbed the walking stick and looked around from left to right. There was a pair of torn rubber slippers. He wore them and came out of the room.

After some thought, he placed the walking stick against the wall and rested his hand on my shoulder.

"You are tall like me. You can support me, right?"

I nodded my head. I began to walk slowly, leading him as if he was my ageing father. When we crossed the hall, the woman began shouting.

"Hey, where are you going? To fall and die in the streets? Listen, just get back in."

He ignored her voice.

"If you go out now, get out forever," she kept yelling.

When we came out, Narasimhan stared at the street, his eyes narrowed and blinking to avoid the glare of the afternoon sun. Clutching on to my shoulder, he said, "It looks like another town. I feel that the street has become smaller."

We started walking down the street. Narasimhan walked very slowly. Ten steps later, he turned back to look at the house.

"I built this house. Now I am scared to even look at it."

Tirugnanam laughed at this. I could not. By the time we came to the end of the road, it was not as hot. Children were going home after school. Loud music blared from the shop at the end of the road.

Narasimhan stood looking at the children with a certain fondness.

"Those who started writing at the same time as I did are all gone. I alone remain. This generation does not know any of us. When we were twenty, we were just like you, talking about poetry endlessly in a rented room in Triplicane. We ran a little magazine. All my poems were published exclusively in that small journal, a *sitridazh*, a zine. No big magazine ever came forward to ask me for a poem. How lovely is this word, 'sitridazh'! Sounds like a wild flower. But sitridazh is really like a small brook. There are some fishes that live only in brooks. If you put them in the sea, they will die. I am like that." He kept looking at the street.

A three-wheel cart carrying gas cylinders passed by. Narasimhan seemed to enjoy the rattling noise made by the cart with childlike glee. Then he turned to Tirugnanam.

"A star keeps shining as revealing itself is what makes it happy. When you come to think of it, a poet is also like that. I am very happy that you all came to see me. I don't want tea, it gives me heartburn. I have wanted to write a poem for a long time, and four lines have just formed in my mind. Shall I say them aloud?"

The poet who had not written anything for twenty years recited three lines in a shaking voice, pouring out what was in his heart, a bubbling stream gushing out of a spring. Then, as he realised that his voice could not be heard clearly against the loud noise from the tea shop, he stopped abruptly.

"Take me home."

I said I will walk back with him and Mohan nodded.

"Don't come and see me like this. It is only when someone comes to see me that I am filled with guilt and regret. Just think that I am dead. That is the best favour you could do me," he told me as he climbed the steps to his house.

When he entered the house, I heard the angry voice of that woman again. Staggering on his unstable legs, Narasimhan went inside.

The Smell of Kerosene

Last night I dreamt about something that happened sixteen years ago. I woke up screaming. My wife who lay beside me was startled.

"What happened?"

For a minute, I could not recognise my room. I did not realise that I was in my bed.

"They have poured kerosene on me." The words came out garbled.

"Who?" she asked, uncomprehending.

"Nothing, nothing. Just some dream," I said.

Half-asleep, I went to the toilet. After peeing, I stood before the mirror. My face looked tense. My heart was still soaked with fear. I smelt my hand, it did not reek of kerosene. *Thank god, I have not been set on fire. I am still alive.* If I had been burnt, I would have been unrecognisable now. Everyone would have forgotten and I would have been an unknown man burnt during the unrest.

I never saw them again, the three young men who poured kerosene on me. What must they be doing now? They must have got married and had children like me. Would they have thought of me ever again? Once in Perambur I saw a man who resembled one of them and I was terrified that it was him. I quickly left on my cycle.

Even today, it is difficult for me to believe that what saved me that night was a glow from a torchlight. Who had shone the torch?

How had he come to be at the bridge exactly at that moment? I could not see the man's face. But it was the light from that faceless man's torch that had saved me. From that day till now, whenever I see light from a torch, I feel a shiver pass through me. Whenever I travel, I carry a torch without fail. I often find myself shining the light from the torch on my palms and then I offer my thanks to the torchlight.

That life-shaking incident happened on 14 June 1997. I was twenty-four, I had just finished my M.Sc. degree and was preparing for banking examinations. At home they insisted that I get a job immediately, so I began teaching maths at a local tutorial college. I had sixty students. Every evening after work, around six-thirty in the evening, I would go to the bridge outside the town limits. Some friends joined me there. We sat chatting late into the night till the second show at the movie theatre got over. Some days I sat there alone till the early hours of the morning.

The bridge was outside the town by the bypass road. Beyond that point, the road was usually empty and there would be just one or two cyclists going towards Sirukulam village. The bridge was built across a small stream. If you stood on the bridge, you could see the highway curving and stretching ahead. There would be a steady flow of trucks carrying goods. As the night grew, the breeze blowing in the outskirts of town changed. Especially, the late-night breeze carried a chill that felt like a rough tickle, like a cow's tongue licking the palm. Sometimes the wind grew stronger and you would feel as if someone was holding you by the scruff of your neck. I have sat there unaware of the time slipping by, just to enjoy the breeze.

During the day, the bridge never looked appealing. It was the evening that gave it its charm, and then it looked beautiful. The bridge was a big part of my life. If I was away from town, I would ask the others and find out who came to the bridge on those days when I was absent, and what they spoke about.

I was always the first to arrive at the bridge. Next came Venkat, who after shutting his flour mill for the day, went home, took a shower, put on a fresh T-shirt and arrived well-combed and smelling of Ponds talcum powder. Once in a while, Appu and Murugan would join us.

We chatted about the girls we loved, movies, apprehensions about the future and general gossip. Sometimes we lit our cigarettes and silently looked at the stars and clouds moving across the sky. Sometimes Appu sang his favourite song aloud:

Naan endraal adu avalum naanum...

Even today, if I hear that song playing somewhere, I cannot but remember Appu.

"Brother, this bridge is like Mohini, like a tempting siren. A man who has sat here once can never free himself from its hold," Murugan said one day.

That was true in my case till that fateful day. But that June 14th destroyed all my fantasies about the bridge. It was a Sunday, and that was the last time I ever sat there.

It was during the period when my town was rife with turmoil and conflict between castes. Five days before, a young man was found dead near the entrance of the bus depot. I too went and saw him.

A thin dark body lay on the ground, with the hands spread out. His dhoti was half-undone at the waist. One blow had fallen at the neck and the other at the waist. The intestines had spilled out, and the blood-soaked ground had changed in colour. Those who had to board the bus took a peek at the dead man and then went about their lives. No one knew who had cut him up. Paying no heed to the corpse there, the juice seller nearby squeezed lime into glasses and added ice cubes...it was business as usual.

When I stood looking at the dead man, I did not know, and there was no indication, that this murder was going to turn everything upside down. The day after this murder, I heard that two load-carrying coolies had been similarly chopped to death near the second railway gate. That evening a crowd gathered with huge wooden poles and went on a rampage breaking and vandalising shops. They said a petrol bunk near the bus depot had been set on fire.

In retaliation, three huts in Fathima Nagar were burnt. The cycle depot near the railway station was also burnt, they said. The reserve police came in vans, and chased away all at sight, attacking them with lathis. The road was strewn with torn slippers, ripped handbags and broken spectacles. A tiffin box had rolled over and fallen in the gutter.

The situation intensified with every passing day. There was no bus service for four days. The bus depot had been shut and a huge tar drum was placed at its entrance. Cinema shows were cancelled. Someone had written "Naayi!" with white limewash on the tar road. Who were they calling a dog? It was not clear. It looked as if some other words had been rubbed away.

During those days the town went quiet earlier than usual. Homes were as quiet as graves. Anyone out on the road on a cycle looked petrified. Two days before, the police went chasing after someone on the street. People said that he had set fire to a mechanic's shed and fled. In the morning, it had burned down to nothing.

They called it a conflict between castes. That was not true. The people had been incited for personal and political gains, the issue of caste was just a façade. The poor commoners of every caste suffered in the conflict manufactured by the *katta* panchayat and wealthy money-lenders.

In five days, eleven persons had been killed. The town was enmeshed in an invisible web of violence. If one saw a person on the road, the mind automatically wondered what caste he belonged to. If two persons were casually chatting, one became suspicious and curious to know if they belonged to the same caste.

The next stage was when people in offices began to openly gather in caste groups. They drew up statistics of caste representation among the residents of each street. Rumours were set afloat that surprise attacks would be launched.

My younger brother, who had till then shown no interest in knowing about our caste, began to proudly display his caste identity ever since the riots started. He also started assembling men who were prepared to attack.

His friend met me one day and said, "Anney, you must gather the boys belonging to our caste who study in your tutorial college. We must also cut up at least four people." He was seething with rage. I had never seen him like that before. I was afraid that something terrible was going to happen.

It is a fallacy that caste does not exist in cities. Caste undergoes a metamorphosis in the cities, it is not as apparent to the eyes there as it is in the villages. But caste is all-pervasive and omnipresent in workplaces, residences, commercial activities, and in marriages and other social customs. Each caste has created its own honcho: for every caste, four or five politicians positioned themselves as caste heroes.

Even schools and colleges have a caste-based hierarchy in their administration. Only after the disturbances began in my town, I understood for the first time that caste oppression manifests in a strange form in cities and towns.

People said that the unrest was deliberately created. They said that when small individual resentments build up, they converge together to blow up, creating a huge uproar. They said it was a power struggle—everyone wanted to take control and settle scores.

I do not know which caste my students who take maths tuition from me belong to. But after the riots began, a student once asked me when he ran into me at the Tilakar Thidal, "It was people from your caste who cut up our man. What do you have to say about that?"

I was blind with rage when I realised that he thought I too was a caste fanatic.

"Have I ever shown my caste leanings?" I burst out angrily.

"But it runs in the blood, doesn't it? Will your caste change just because you say so?" he retorted and rode away on his cycle.

I could not comprehend why people felt so strongly about caste, how it polarised people so quickly. Though I was aware of caste differences, I did not know how capable it was of taking lives.

Normal life in the town had collapsed. Someone had killed Ratnasami, the peon at the Taluk office. His daughter was seen screaming and wailing on the streets. There was no sign of rituals taking place in the house of mourning, and no one went to offer their condolences.

Even in this tense situation, I continued to go the bridge and chat with my friends. The unrest had brought about many changes in our town.

"Something good has come out of this turmoil. Until yesterday people would shout and make a fuss if they were asked to get off the bus outside the bus depot. Today they were asked to get off at the corner about two miles away, and yet, not a whisper, *da*! All of them got down quietly and walked the distance. This unrest has taught us many lessons," Appu remarked.

Natarajan replied, "You will laugh if you hear this. There was an old stick at home, a pointed one, a *velkambu*. Now my family has wiped it clean and kept it near the door. It seems a weapon is needed as a safeguard now."

I was even more shocked and confused on hearing this. Was it really so easy to make a town insane? Why have people become so violent and fierce? I felt a fear deepening inside me.

June 14th. At seven in the evening, there was a total power failure across town. I rode my cycle to the bridge and sat there. I could see numerous trucks moving in a line on the highway. The friends who usually joined me were not to be seen...not one of them was there that evening.

I sat in the dark lost in thought. Suddenly a headlight from a motorcycle flashed on my face. Someone must be coming to sit here at the bridge, I thought. The motorbike slowed down and stopped nearby.

Three men were seated on it. Two of them wore lungis. They must have been about twenty. I thought perhaps they were looking for a place to sit and drink. The motorbike started again and moved southwards.

It stopped a hundred feet away from the bridge. One man got down and walked towards the shrubs. Maybe to piss, I thought. Then they rode away and the motorbike disappeared out of my sight.

There was no wind at all. The air was humid as though it was going to rain. I thought it might be better to go home, have a bath and sleep on the terrace. But I remembered that I would have to hand-pump the water for my bath, and this thought made me annoyed. And the pump would make a loud noise—*keech keech*! After I start working, with my first salary I must get a shower fitted in the bathroom, I thought. My thoughts wandered as I began speculating where and in which town I might find employment.

I noticed that the highway was suddenly empty, no truck was going to and fro. But I knew that in a short while fourteen or fifteen of them would arrive all at once.

It was a puzzle, I told myself.

The motorbike that had gone past me returned and stopped near the bridge once more. One of the men got down. He came up, lit a cigarette and looked at me.

"What do you want?" I asked softly.

"Which area are you from?" His voice was rough.

"Melatheru," I said. He staggered towards the other two and said something. Then they all got down from the bike.

I stood up as they came near me. The one who wore pants asked me, "What are you?"

I did not reply.

"I asked, which caste?" He glared at me.

"Why should I tell you? I belong to this town, and that's all you need to know."

"Son of a bitch! Just set him aflame and we will move on. Dey, Rangu, hold him tight." He ordered in a firm voice.

As I tried to get away on my cycle a hand grabbed me by the scruff of my neck and pushed me down. My cycle clattered to the ground. Another man leapt on me and tied my feet with a rope as I kept struggling. As I shouted in pain, another stuffed a dirty cloth into my mouth. I continued to struggle, trying to free myself of the binds.

The one wearing trousers stamped on my face and said, "Bring the kerosene tin, brother."

"Are we really going to set him on fire?" one of them asked.

"Let's do it. Who will know *we* did it? Let one dog die at our hands."

One went to get the kerosene tin.

I am going to die. They are going to burn me alive, I thought. I trembled with fear as my eyes filled with tears.

The one who had gone away on the motorbike came back with a tin of kerosene. As one of them had his foot pressed against my face, it was impossible for me to raise my head. The other held me down firmly. The man who brought the tin emptied the contents all over me.

I tasted kerosene for the first time as it flowed over my face. Then it spread under my shirt and over my legs.

As the man in trousers bent over me with a cigarette lighter, some passing cyclist on the Sirukulam road flashed his torch at us.

The man with the lighter did not light the fire. He turned around.

"Hey! Who is there?" A loud voice came from the direction of the torchlight. I did not know who the cyclist was. But when the three men heard the voice, they fled towards the south.

The man who had flashed the torch did not come to the bridge. Maybe he too had shouted in fear. I lay there drenched in kerosene, saved from death by a hair's breadth. The flow of trucks had resumed on the highway.

Early next morning the man who delivered milk from Sirukulam saw me lying there tied up. When he set me free, I cried like a child.

"Thambi, who did this?" he asked, agitated.

I could not speak a word.

He was terrified and anxious.

"Where is your house? I will take you home."

"No, Annachi. I will go myself." I looked at my cycle, it was lying near the *thumbai* shrub.

As I rode back to town on my cycle and saw the familiar streets, shops, and people—everything filled me with fear. The smell of kerosene floating around me was like the stench of death. I did not tell anyone at home what had happened.

For ten days I just lay at home and did not go out.

Who were they? Why did they try to kill me?

It was their first attempt at murder. Was it just a game for them?

If they had indeed killed me, what would have happened?

As these thoughts plagued my mind, sleep deserted me.

I left the town as I felt I could no longer live there. I moved to Chennai. Even today, that incident remains a raw wound that has never healed. I often feel as if I am burning.

I cannot live with caste pride. But I also cannot shrug off my caste identity completely. All that I can do is live on, suppressing my caste. I will never be free from the shackles of caste. And this saddens me deeply.

The light that the hands of that anonymous man had shone on me that night, I see as the universe's all-encompassing compassion.

I will never know whose hands they were. But I kneel down in gratitude every day and I pray to him...that faceless voice, those hands and that light that saved me.

The House Where No One Lived

It was not dawn yet. People were walking inside Vadamedu Estate. The early hours of the morning have a special beauty during winter: a dense fog like a flowing river, drops of mist covering the tea shrubs, a tiny yellow light sparkling from the supervisor's house on the slope of the hill, the silhouetted trees, their tops hidden and lanes veiled in fog.

Moosa was in his khaki trousers and woollen sweater, with a muffler tied round his head. He was about forty-five years old and less than four and a half feet tall. He was born with a limp: a shorter right leg that made him drag his feet as he walked.

His boss, Pilathu *Muthalali*, was tall. He looked like a theatre actor from old times. He was wearing a dhoti and a red sweater, and had fully covered himself with a blue shawl. He wore heavy footwear that looked like military boots and even though he was past seventy, he did not need glasses.

"If you have fish thrice a day, your sight will never fail you," he often said, and he had to have fish thrice a day. Without the smell of fish, food was not food to him. His breakfast was always tapioca and fish. His wife teased him that he must have been a stork in his previous life.

They lived in the estate bungalow until six years ago. It was only after their first son got married that they moved to the town.

But, thrice a week, Pilathu still came and stayed in the estate. He muttered to himself, "How can a man sleep without the fragrance of tea?" As he grew older, sleep grew more distant from him. Even if he went to bed at nine, he kept tossing and turning. If one kept two pillows on the bed, the mind believed that there would be someone for company, and it would wait for them, refusing to fall asleep. How easily the mind is deceived! Near his bed was a time-piece bought in Singapore. He would hold it in his hand and watch the time tick by. When he was twenty, the early morning sun was his alarm clock. He always woke up before sunrise. It is only now at this age that he needed the alarm.

Darkness spread across the hills like a thick wet blanket. It was not so thick in the town, the darkness. Light kept leaking into the night like sunlight through an umbrella with holes. But the night that covered the hills, especially in the rainy season, would fill men with fear.

Pilathu was used to these hills and the nights. He knew this moaning wind, the riotous dancing trees, and the sun that glowed early in the morning clearing away all traces of the night. The blooming flowers, the lush green shrubs radiating freshness along the lanes, the insects that clung to the shrubs and the birds perched on branches screeching to break out of their languor...he knew them all. Sometimes at dawn, it seemed as though his heart was clasped by an overwhelming sadness. Try as he might he could not find out the cause of his melancholy. Maybe when people grow old, all the sorrows that have lain buried for years combine as one. It felt as if a huge iron ball was pressing down on his chest.

The pain would vanish only on seeing the sun. So he began to spread his arms wide every morning to gather its warmth. He rubbed the sunlight on his face. How can one live in this estate without indulging oneself with the sunlight? The sun was their grandfather, a rough old man staggering around like a drunkard. Sometimes Pilathu stood near the lake's edge looking at the western sky as the sun gradually set. Just like his grandfather, his *thatha,* the sun would slowly walk, supporting itself on the shoulders of the wind before disappearing out of sight. Today the sun was still not to be seen. Maybe it was also feeling lazy this chilly morning.

They climbed up the mound while it was still dark. This mound used to be higher once. But they had chipped away to make it flatter. Jones *Durai*'s horse climbed this mound leaping. One day it tripped and fell here. Jones, who was riding it, fell down, broke his hip and had to be taken to the hospital. It was only after this incident that they sent some men and levelled the mound.

Every place where man sets his foot becomes a memory. Every tree, ditch and curve in this estate has its own story. The large grassy stretch on the slope too...it was made for Jones to play on. The sun grazed on this grass stretch like a solitary cow.

The chilly wind froze the tip of his nose. A nameless insect chirped, "kut kut". Carrying memories with them, they walked on.

The mist wiped Pilathu's face clean. The air was thick with the smell of tea that grew in shrubs all around them. The dense smell spread in the dark, denser than the smell of *thazhampoo,* a smell he loved. They breathed it in as they walked up the mound. Moosa was short of breath, but he kept walking without letting on. Who else would have the privilege of walking with Pilathu Muthalali? How many years have they walked like this? Moosa thought as he leaned on his knees to make the climb easier. His knees ached. He must rub oil and massage them as soon as he went home. He realised that his legs were growing weak. If walking became impossible, then he could no longer live in the hills, he would have to descend to the plains.

Pilathu Muthalali spoke as they walked on the path that led towards the east.

"Moosa, I have a wish to build a house on top of Pulikuthipaarai. By house, I don't mean a small house but a big bungalow...a house with a hundred windows."

"Muthalali, why do you need a hundred windows in a house on top of the hill? Even if you have just four windows, won't the wind rush in?"

"*Illey da,* Moosa! A hundred there must be. When I was young, whenever I entered a house, I would count the windows. I have seen homes with four, six, twelve, eighteen windows! I once went to a bungalow in Hyderabad that had sixty-four windows. But all of them were kept shut. It seemed they opened it only on New Year's Day. And when they did, the light would just flood in. I wanted to spend at least one day there, da Moosa. But it was a Muslim gentleman's house, how could he let me stay? I just stared and stared and then came back. This was almost thirty years ago. Since that day I have had this wish to somehow build a house with a hundred windows."

"You have all the money to build it, Muthalali. If you want to, you can build it in the town itself."

"It's not like that, Moosa. The houses in the town are like coffins. Look at my own bungalow there. It is a three-storeyed house on a four-ground plot. But when my car stops at the porch, I resent having to enter the wretched thing. But Pilathu Muthalali is a millionaire. Can he just spread a mat in front of the house and lie down there, you tell me? When I came here long ago as a young coolie, I would lie down like that. And when it rained, I didn't have a shelter. I would stay awake till it stopped raining and then spread the gunny bag on the wet ground and lie down. And it was such pleasure, Moosa! A man who has tasted the joy of lying on wet ground will not lust after a woman, I tell you."

Moosa laughed.

"Why do you laugh? It is true. This wetness, you know, is not an ordinary thing. It feels as if the damp ground is gently pressing against you. It is impossible to describe in words the joy you feel when the cool dampness of the ground touches your abdomen. You must feel it, experience it yourself. My wife scolds me, she says that if

I sleep with my belly to the floor like that, my limbs will be affected. But I love a wet floor."

"Muthalali, you have sandalwood cots and plush mattresses at home. Why should you lie on the wet floor? That is only for those chaps who have nothing."

"I too came here to this estate as a chap with nothing. You won't remember. It was Umaru Muthalali who owned the estate to the north then. Do you know what he looked like? A golden complexion like the famous M.G.R., and if you went close to him, you could smell the fragrance of attar. He always had a Ceylon umbrella in his hand and a cheroot in his pocket. He smoked only cheroots. He had three wives. But he was always around in the estate. It was he who called me one day and said, 'Pilathu, for all your toils in this forest, you must get some reward. Tell you what, take this land lying bare to the east. Dig it up—get some men to help you, and plant tea. You plant tea anywhere on these hills, it will grow. I'll tell the durai and get you the land. If you tend to those plants with as much care as you would give a girl child, one day you too will become a muthalali.'

"I did not believe his words then. But it was Umaru Muthalali who helped me get this land. However, he did not pay even a paisa. I plucked tea leaves and sold them to earn the money needed to buy the land. For some reason Umaru Muthalali took a liking to me. I really don't know why."

"How can you say that, Muthalali? It is all because of your goodness, your good virtues. So many people you have helped! When my mother was ill, it was you who gave me the money to take her to Madurai for treatment. You have given money to help so many people without sparing a thought."

"Money comes and goes, Moosa. What I did is not a big deal. But Umaru Muthalali saw something else in me. Every man has unknown to him a rare quality. That can only be discovered by someone else, we ourselves do not know what it is. Hasn't the

Creator made us in such a way that we cannot see our own back? Only another man can."

"What is there on our backs, Muthalali?"

"Not like that, da. The back never grows old. Just notice a woman's back when she walks. You can never guess her age. Our back does not age."

"So true, Muthalali! Even I have been deceived sometimes."

Pilathu Muthalali laughed with Moosa. They had by then walked all the way up to Irattai Thotti Street. Now they just had to go back home. The sun had not risen yet, it liked to sleep in a little bit longer in the winter. Just like people. Perhaps the sun's long association with humans had made it as languid as them.

Pilathu Muthalali was lost in his thoughts about building the house, he did not utter a word thereafter. Moosa walked along quietly. As they approached the estate bungalow, they saw that the dog had been let loose. It romped about and sprinted happily towards them.

"Did you give him biscuits?" Pilathu asked, stroking the dog's head.

The worker-woman nodded. Pilathu was strict when it came to caring for dogs. They must be given meat and biscuits on time. He had appointed one person just to take care of the dogs.

Moosa shook the dew drops off his hair as he walked towards his home. Muthalali would summon him again only at night. He liked to chat with Moosa for a while before going to sleep. Sometimes he would ask Moosa to sleep in the bungalow, and Moosa would lie down in the hall. In spite of knowing Muthalali for so many years, Moosa could never understand him.

When summer set in, Pilathu Muthalali invited Father Joseph to Pulikuthipaarai to conduct a service and offer the Eucharist, asking for the Lord's blessings to commence construction. His wife and children were angry with him for this plan to build a house on top of the hill. He paid scant regard to them.

It is not an easy task to build a house on top of a mountain. Moreover, there were no proper roads in the Pulikuthipaarai area. One had to climb the steep rock on foot, so they loaded the materials on donkeys who carried them up. It was difficult to find workers because Pilathu was firm on his decision to use only stones and no bricks.

The construction work would pause if it rained. He had tents put up for the workers where they could take shelter during the rain. But he would be after them as soon as the skies cleared. The house came up little by little. He paid the workers twice the usual rate and made them work from six in the morning to nine at night. Even when they were busy at work, he stood nearby, yelling at them. The chief engineer Henry, who came from the town, and his assistants mentally cursed Pilathu Muthalali. Money was spent like water.

One day Moosa said, "Muthalali, even Jones Durai did not build a hilltop bungalow like this. If you live here, you will be like a king."

"This house is not for me to live in, Moosa."

"What do you mean, Muthalali?"

"Yes, da Moosa. No one should live in that house. Let the house be alone by itself, just like Pulikuthipaarai. We can go to the house whenever we want and enjoy the wind, have a chat, but never live there. Let it remain the house where no one ever lived."

"I don't understand, Muthalali. Don't people build houses to live in, with their family?"

"You won't understand, Moosa. Let the house be completed. Then you yourself will say that no one is deserving enough to live in such a house. This hill has given me an abundance of gifts, so I am gifting a house to it in return."

"For whom?"

"Let the wind, the sunshine, the frost and the moonlight live there, Moosa."

"Why spend so much on a house where you are not going to live? This house has already gobbled up so much money."

"I would like people to say, 'Pilathu Muthalali built a house, but he did not live there. He just left it like the trees he planted.'"

"Muthalali, you must not build a house and leave it like that. It will punish the man who built it and will not let him live."

"That can't be true, Moosa. Little children build sand-houses, and they look lovely, but does anyone live in them? Just like the children build sandcastles for their own sake, I am building this house for its own sake, all right?"

"I just don't understand you, Muthalali."

"Leave it. Don't breathe a word about this till the house is completed."

And Moosa did not. But he really hated it when he saw the house being built. He cursed it calling it a poisonous tree. When the house built of black stones with its hundred windows stood complete, it looked like an eagle with its wings spread wide.

Pilathu stood near the completed house, running his hand along the stone walls. He would murmur gently with his face to the stones as though he was speaking to a child. Even when he was unwell, he would walk around the house, coughing. The people in the hills kept talking about the house that Pilathu Muthalali built. Even his wife Lissy and his son-in-law who came to see the stone house had never imagined that he would be able to build a house of such exquisite beauty.

The windows were wide, really wide. No one in the hills had a house with so many windows. The supervisor said it would be impossible to live in this house in winter. The women workers who came to clean the house were wonderstruck.

Pilathu had undergone a transformation by the time the house was complete. He spoke less and less. He did not talk even during their morning walks and looked lost in thought. Some days he went to sleep by six in the evening. Some days he ate just the kanji and left the fish untouched.

The house that Pilathu Muthalali built quickly became a unique landmark. Workers came by just to stand and gaze at it. The house was not fully ready yet, some carvings were still being made and decorative door handles were to be fitted.

After two and a half years, it was finally ready. When Father Joseph said that there should be a big banquet for the housewarming, Pilathu said, "No, Father, I am not going to live there."

"Then? Are you planning to rent it out? Who will come to live in this huge house on a hill?"

"No, Father, no one is ever going to live in this house. I had a desire to build a house like this, that's all. Let there be one house in this world where no man ever lived."

"What stupidity, Pilathu!" Father Joseph was annoyed.

"The Taj Mahal that Shahjahan built spending crores and crores was not a house for him to live in. Inside it lies his wife's coffin. Who spends so much for a dead wife? The world calls such a fellow a fool. But isn't it Shahjahan's name, Father, that still lives in our memory? There will not be a grave as beautiful as the Taj Mahal in a hundred lifetimes. This Pilathu too is a crazy fellow like Shahjahan, Father," said Pilathu, laughing. Father Joseph did not get it.

Pilathu and Moosa were having drinks that night.

"Tomorrow, you and I will inaugurate the new house and welcome the sun inside," Pilathu said.

They drank all night. Moosa sang.

Early next day they walked towards Thattamparai with the iron key. The house with a hundred windows glowed in the gentle light of the morning.

"Moosa, see how beautiful it is! When I first came here, I was a nobody. I did not have even a fistful of sand to call my own. It is this hill that has showered so much wealth on me. To return its gift, I have built this house for the hill. Yes, da Moosa. This house belongs to this hill. Let the sun and the moon live here. Let the wind and the rain take rest inside. Let light and darkness play around. The hundred windows are not to make the house beautiful. It is to show that the man who built it is magnanimous. As the wind blows through the hundred windows, the heart feels lighter and lighter. Do you know how many days I have wept on this mountain because there was no one around for me? It was the wind then that stroked my head and said, 'I am here for you, I am here.' It is this hill that has reared and nurtured me."

Moosa was shaken to hear Pilathu sob. They opened the door and went inside. They threw open all the windows. The light of the early morning sun filled the house. Pilathu knelt in front of the house and offered his thanks to Christ.

Moosa's wonder grew and grew as he kept looking at that house. Why have such intricate workmanship and so many rooms in a house where no one would live? Not one word passed between the two. They stayed there in that house till the sun rose high. Pilathu asked Moosa not to close any of the windows. They just shut the main door and returned to the estate bungalow.

Word spread all around the hill that Pilathu built a house and left it unoccupied. People came in droves to see the house of solitude with its hundred windows. They yearned and sighed and wished that they could live there. Some chided Pilathu for having lost his mind. Pilathu didn't give a hoot about what people said. His wife, daughter, son-in-law and other members of his family thought they could somehow move in to the house by persuading him. But Pilathu stood firm in his resolve.

He went to the house once every day and just stood there. Some days he would sit on the steps. No one but him was allowed to go inside.

Pilathu fell ill six months after the house was complete. One night he asked for the door to be opened and then he went in and stood in the dark hall. That was his last visit to the house. Two days later he died.

Pilathu had left a will in which he had mentioned clearly that no one should live in that house and that none of his heirs could claim right to it.

The sun and the wind ruled the house where no man lived. The rain snuck in through the windows. The birds peeped inside and cats became house-guests. In the winter, the cold and frost filled all the rooms one after the other. Water seeped in. Plants sprouted. Insects multiplied. The house stood alone on top of the hill—it was as if Pilathu himself was standing there. Time gradually changed the appearance of the beautiful house: moss covered the stones, the doors developed cracks and weeds covered the floor. Even then, the people of the neighbouring hills would refer to it as the house that Pilathu built. The girl who drove the grazing cattle said that sometimes the house stared fixedly like a one-eyed man.

Moosa did not go there at all after Pilathu had passed away. Once the house had appeared in his dream where it swayed to and fro like a swing.

Many years later, Moosa, who had grown old and weak, came to Kuthiraimedu and looked at the dilapidated house from a distance. The wild wind and the incessant rain that lived in the house had eventually plucked the door out. The house stood in ruins, its windows too snatched and flung away. It looked as if Pilathu Muthalali was standing there rain-drenched, his head bent down and arms spread wide.

"Why did he build a house like this? What fool builds a house with a hundred windows and not live there? What kind of madness is that?"

Moosa was filled with a helpless sorrow. He moved closer to the house and noticed that thick weeds had grown all over it. It was a house where no one had ever lived. No one had ever spent a single night there.

The house of solitude had now aged. It was feeble and ravaged. Like a human being, a house too grows old; it appears in this world, lives for a while and then departs.

"Muthalali, no one can ever be as large-hearted as you were."

Unbidden tears filled his eyes as Moosa folded his hands in reverence and looked up at the house of solitude that had a hundred windows.

The Death of Thidiyan

To the east of Veeranur was a small hillock and a temple. You cannot really call it a temple—it was a small altar in a tiny room, that was all. They called it Thidiyan *kovil* or Thidiyan temple. When one asked who Thidiyan was, they said that he was a farmer who lived in the village. After he was horribly murdered, the temple was built in his memory where his descendants worshipped him and offered prayers every year.

The sun shone brightly on the hillock. Before Thidiyan went there to cultivate the land, no one lived in that area. The villagers said that long, long ago there was a spring on top of the hillock, but as the days passed it dried up. No one knew why Thidiyan lived outside the village in that place.

Martin Devasagayam had now purchased the land and the hillock next to Thidiyan temple. It was for his sake that I was there to survey the land and mark it with stones. Though my job was to survey lands, I loved listening to stories during my off-duty hours.

I had been there three days and every day someone or the other kept talking about Thidiyan. So I began to piece together all the different bits of information that I could gather about him from the shared memories of many.

The temple *poosari*, the priest, Muniyandi, was the first to recall these stories. He began with how Thidiyan died. It is strange that people remember how a man died better than how he had lived. It was so in the case of Thidiyan too.

Thidiyan had been stabbed by an unknown young man near Mottaiparai, the bald, barren rock on the other side of this same hillock around two in the afternoon. Thidiyan was then seventy-six. He lay there, his hair dusty red, his nails dirty, and his feet unshod. The twisted veins on his hands looked like crawling worms.

No one had seen the young man who killed Thidiyan ever before. He had stabbed Thidiyan in his abdomen and thighs, and after Thidiyan fell down, he had stabbed the soles of his feet. If he wished he could have aimed for Thidiyan's heart, but none of the stabs were on the upper part of the body. The assailant had chopped off a bunch of hair from Thidiyan's head. No one knew why.

Muniyandi said that Thidiyan must have had wronged some family and this was the punishment.

The young man who killed Thidiyan had stood near the rock until Thidiyan breathed his last. Before he died, Thidiyan had stared at the young man as if wanting to say something, but then his head drooped and he died. Then the young man came to the village and told them he had killed old Thidiyan, and that it was the punishment Thidiyan deserved. He then left the place.

For a long time, the villagers thought that the young man was Thidiyan's illegitimate son, and that he fought with his father for his share of the land and eventually killed him. But Thidiyan's eldest daughter Thangam said that this could not have been the case. It was true that her father had two relationships with women in two places but neither of them had a son. If that was true, why did this young man kill Thidiyan? People were puzzled. Because of his unnatural death, Thidiyan had become the perpetual topic of discussion in the village.

The villagers believed that two days after Thidiyan died, the spring got blocked and water stopped flowing, so it must have been Thidiyan's spirit that blocked the spring.

I did not know what he looked like because there were no photographs. From what people described, I guessed that Thidiyan would have been less than five and a half feet tall. But he had a sturdy frame. He could wolf down four big jugs of *kanji* for one meal. A guzzler with a wolf's stomach he really was with his bottomless appetite. His eyes were a jaundiced yellow, and he was always roaming about.

According to Pethayya Naicker, Thidiyan had probably joined as a labourer at Reddiar's house when he was a twelve-year-old boy to herd the cattle. Reddiar had many cows in his cowshed. All day Thidiyan remained in that shed, scooping the cow dung and dropping it in the manure pit, making dung-cakes with the fresh dung, washing the cows and taking them out to graze.

Thidiyan is not a name that is common among those living in these *karisal* lands where the soil is black. He might have come from the north. The workers in Reddiar's house were given only one meal a day, and that too at noon. They would make the workers sit down in the thatched backyard and give them horse-millet or rye. There would be no food at night. If they ate well and slept, then they would not want to get up early in the morning to work as they would be sleepy. Only a hungry person would rise early and go to work. This was Siddu Reddiar's thinking.

He had more than thirty labourers. Thidiyan rose early in the morning, went to the cowshed, cleared loads and loads of cow dung, and bathed the cattle. Then he brought the *konaar*, the man who milked the cows, saw to it that all the cows were milked, cut grass and spread it before the cows, ground the oilcake feed, and carefully removed the ticks from each cow. He would drown himself in his chores.

He never ate with the other labourers. He always ate alone, and it was always Nachiyar who gave him his food. He literally kept shovelling the food in, without lifting his head, until Nachiyar carried the empty pot away, indicating he had eaten enough and there was no more. Only then would he get up. He cared little if the others mocked the way he ate.

Some days when there was too much of the stale gruel left over, they would give the whole pot to him. He would polish off all of it by himself and give the pot back after washing it. On those days, Chinna Avva, the elderly matriarch of the house, would scold him and call him Wolf Belly. He laughed it away, saying, "I eat to fill my belly. Why should I be scolded for that?"

Thidiyan's hunger could never be appeased. Even if he had just finished eating, he could readily sit down to eat again if someone asked. He had *that* much hunger. Nachiyar would say, "The woman who marries you will be unable to feed you full and run away. Eat a little less!"

"I won't marry a woman who cannot fulfil my hunger."

Nachiyar would laugh at that. In Reddiar's household, it was Nachiyar whom Thidiyan worshipped as though she were a deity.

On occasion Nachiyar gave Thidiyan some palm jaggery and groundnuts to eat. When Nachiyar went to the Vadakkampatti temple, it was Thidiyan who drove the cart. Once Thidiyan went somewhere and got peacock blood for Nachiyar. She was mighty pleased. Once he even got her some *kaattu elandai*, a kind of wild jujube.

Thidiyan had no interest in bathing or combing his hair. If he felt itchy, he would rush to the pond where the buffaloes bathed, take four or five dips and come away. He never wiped his body dry. When he walked back to the village with a damp head of hair and his well-toned body wet and glistening, the women would giggle. Thidiyan never looked at the women nor did he speak to them.

Once Reddiar's red cow was about to calve, but the calf's head turned inside the mother and it was stuck, unable to come out. The cow cried in pain until she was exhausted. After struggling all night, they could pull the calf out. But it was born dead. Though the cow knew that her calf was dead, she kept licking it. The cow's eyes were wet and she moaned weakly in pain. Thidiyan broke down when he saw this. Tears streamed down his face and he beat his chest.

"Yamma...! Yamma...!"

When they saw him cry like this, the women around were heart-broken and began sobbing too. Only then they got to know that Thidiyan had lost his mother as a child. His wail for a mother's love won the hearts of all the women in the house. Nachiyar gave Thidiyan some raw eggs to drink, and Thidiyan always did as she said.

One time the mud wall of the cowshed collapsed when it rained incessantly for four days. Not knowing where to house the cattle, they quickly put up a makeshift thatched shed on top of the hillock and moved the cows there. That is how Thidiyan came to be at that place near the hillock. Since Siddu Reddiar's house was far from the hillock, no one came looking for him. After milking the cows, it was Thidiyan himself who took the milk to Reddiar's house.

When Thidiyan moved to this hillock after having been confined within Reddiar's cowshed all these years, something changed in him. During the day he would come out and climb up the hillock to sit on the round rock. He sat staring at the village sloping down the east, at the fields; he watched the men returning home after work as did the flocks of birds. Even though Siddu Reddiar scolded him for doing this, Thidiyan could not resist going up the hillock to gaze around. Whenever he had some time, he climbed up to the top.

One day, just before the summer started, Thidiyan came to Siddu Reddiar's house and said that he wanted to be paid for the work he had done all these years. It was the custom to measure out *kambu* and ragi in lieu of cash for the work done by the labourers at Reddiar's.

"You are asking for money at a time when there has been no yield. We will see in the month of Chitrai. Go now!" Siddu Reddiar glared at Thidiyan.

"Then give me a cow, and I will earn my living on my own."

"What will you do with one cow?"

"I'm going to level the lands to the west of the hillock and grow crops there."

"That is an arid, scorched land with red soil. Who would want to try farming there? Have you lost your mind? Go...go and do your work in the cowshed."

"No, *Emman*. I want to earn my living with my own hands," Thidiyan said, his head bowed.

Siddu Reddiar grew angry.

"You will get nothing from me, not even a bit of shit. Go away!"

That night Thidiyan chose a strong red bull from Reddiar's cowshed and left the village with it. When Siddu Reddiar found out, he jumped up and down with rage, and sent his men to get the thieving Thidiyan back. It was Chinna Avva who pacified him.

"Let that ass go. Let him survive elsewhere if he can. At least you don't have to pay him anything now."

Siddu Reddiar did his calculation and felt that one bull was not that high a price for nine years of hard labour, and so he let the matter go.

No one knew where Thidiyan went and what he did. But when he returned, he was accompanied by a tall woman. She had a statuesque figure that shone like a well-oiled black *dhal*.

When he left the village, Thidiyan was always in shorts. But now he wore a dhoti and a brown shirt.

"Who is this, Thidiya? Your wife? You found someone who agreed to give his daughter to you? What caste is she?" Nachiyar asked sharply.

"She is a labourer like me. She came to me, trusting me, and I accepted her. Only a rock can support another rock," Thidiyan replied respectfully.

Nachiyar kept staring at her.

"Let me see. Ask her to turn around and let her hair loose."

Thidiyan's wife stood still.

"Poncholai, untie your hair, Ma," Thidiyan said gently.

Poncholai unfurled her thick hair. It flowed like a black cascade and touched her heels. Nachiyar was eaten up by jealousy and kept staring.

"Thidiya, your wife has ankle-length hair. Such long hair does not suit one who does manual labour. It is said that a woman with heel-length hair has uncontrolled sexual desires and will run away with another man. First thing first, cut her hair till above the waist."

"No, Amma. She tends to it with loving care. Why should it be cut?"

"What impertinence! Do as I say!" Nachiyar snapped.

"Please, anything but that...please, Thaayaaramma," Thidiyan folded his hands and pleaded. Whenever he became emotional, he would call Nachiyar "Thaayaaramma" or Mother.

"*Ennada,* ey! Are you dancing to the tune of your new bride now? I am ordering you, chop it!"

"Please, Thaayaaramma. Let her be...she's just a young girl," Thidiyan begged.

"Why have anything to do with that bastard? Chase him away," Siddu Reddiar told his wife.

"You heard what he said, didn't you? Why are you still standing here, Thidiya? I took care of you like my child...Now this bitch from nowhere has changed you."

Thidiyan was calm.

"Why are you still standing here?" Nachiyar asked.

"I went away without getting my pay for nine years of labour. If you give me what I am owed, two lives will be able to survive."

"I shall hit with you a slipper! You stole the bull and now you have the guts to ask for pay. If I see you again in this village, I will bury you alive," Reddiar shouted.

"That is not fair, Muthalali. Then I will have to complain to the village panchayat," Thidiyan said, his head bent.

When she heard these words, Nachiyar lost her temper. She rushed inside the house and came out with the sickle used to cut paddy. She grabbed Pooncholai's hair and chopped it off like a tuft of rush and threw the bunch of hair away.

"Go and add this to your complaint to the panchayat. Let us see what verdict they give."

Pooncholai stood trembling. Thidiyan picked up the bunch of cut hair and strode out with his wife.

He did not seek justice from any panchayat.

"You will let your hair grow out only when we are able to hold our heads high in this place. My resolve will remain strong if I see your hair in a state like this."

Pooncholai did not disagree. Thidiyan and his wife toiled and made the barren land near the hillock fit for cultivation. Thidiyan had grown corn. Thidiyan often remembered with anguish how Nachiyar behaved with them—Nachiyar, whom he had worshipped like his mother! He just could not comprehend why women's love grew bitter.

Sometimes when Thidiyan's wife went to the town to buy groceries, the children would jeer at her. "Hey *mottachi*! Mottachi! Baldie!" they would say. Sometimes even the shopkeeper would ask her, "What does mottachi want?" No one in the village knew who had cut her hair.

The land did not bear as much crop as Thidiyan expected. What they got from the harvest was just enough for the two of them.

There was no rain for two years. The village wells went dry and there was a drought so harsh that the village even ran out of drinking water. During this drought and famine, Thidiyan's wife delivered a child. Starved and parched, her frail body lay on the mat, her breasts dry and devoid of milk. Every day people kept leaving the village hoping to find some work somewhere. Even the people who were well-off decided not to remain there and moved to Thanjavur. Unable to bear the scorching heat, Thidiyan's child died in ten days. He buried the child near the rock on the left side of the hillock. He could not even weep for his child, his eyes were so dry.

Thidiyan's wife asked him if they should also leave the place and seek work elsewhere.

"No. Even if we must die, we will die here," Thidiyan said firmly.

Thidiyan's wife asked her brother to come and take her two children away one night. Then it was only Thidiyan and his wife alone who remained there on top of the hillock, looking ruefully at the village desiccated by the hot wind. The entire village had been transformed into a graveyard. Only forty families remained. If they too died, the village would be completely desolate.

One day Thidiyan saw a slight trace of water on the rock on top of the hillock. He began to break the rock, trying to move it, hoping to find the source of the water. But the rock was hard and firm in its place.

The husband and wife kept chipping at the rock day and night. That noise was like a toll warning the village. One evening Thidiyan got fed up with everything and he lay down by the rock wailing. "Why am I stuck with this wretched thing?" he cried. Even in the dead of the night, his wife continued to chip away at the rock. After a few days, as Thidiyan tapped the rock hard, it broke and water from a deep spring gushed forth. He was filled with wonder on seeing that even in this drought, water could flow from a rock. He cupped some water in his palms and tasted it. It was sweet. He then called the entire village and showed them the spring. Men and women began to crowd around the spring for water.

Thidiyan's wife said, "No one can take this water for free. For one pot of water, you must give two measures of kambu or ragi. Water only for the man who has grain."

Since it was an impossibility to find water elsewhere, people began to buy the water in exchange for two measures of grain. The husband and wife slept next to the rock like guardians of the spring.

The spring water flowed unceasingly. Once late at night, in the dark, Thidiyan saw a woman stealthily take some water and hastily rush down the slope. He could not see her face. He rushed through a shortcut and accosted her.

It was Siddu Reddiar's wife, Nachiyar.

As soon as she saw Thidiyan she shrank.

"Some drinking water...that's why..." she mumbled.

"Why are you slinking in the dark for that, Ma?" Thidiyan asked.

Pooncholai who had followed Thidiyan came and stood before Nachiyar. She glared at her and said, "Hey, put the pot down! If you want water, I will take your hair as payment. Is that all right?"

When she heard this, Nachiyar looked at Thidiyan and said,

"Thidiya, how often have I fed you with this hand? Have you forgotten that? Are you really this ungrateful?"

"It is only because of that that I am asking you just for a bunch of hair, and nothing more," Thidiyan's wife said.

Nachiyar pleaded, "Just one pot of water, please, I beg of you. I will give you my earrings instead."

"A bunch of your hair for a pot of water, or else you can drink your piss and die," Thidiyan's wife said.

"Thidiya, did I feed you and raise you to become this?" Nachiyar sobbed pathetically.

"We want no drama, no tears. Put the pot down," Thidiyan's wife said sternly.

Nachiyar lowered the pot and knelt before Thidiyan.

"Don't do this, Thidiya. This sin will haunt you forever."

Thidiyan took the knife tucked at this waist and chopped Nachiyar's hair. A thick clump of hair fell at her feet. Nachiyar did not shed a tear. As she was going away with the pot of water, she said, "Thidiya, one day you will suffer for disfiguring me like this."

Thidiyan just laughed. Pooncholai waved the clump of hair in the wind and danced joyously. Her laughter could be heard from the hillock; it sounded like the wail of a beast.

Next morning, Siddu Reddiar and Nachiyar disappeared from the village, leaving Chinna Avva alone in that house. When Thidiyan went to their house, Chinna Avva, who had gone blind, pleaded, "Thidiya, it has been ten days since I had a bath. Please give me a bath with the spring water."

"That...we will do on the day we have to bury you. Where is the master? He is not to be seen anywhere."

"They left for Vadamalaikurichi in the night itself. It seems they will never return to this village. I won't have a soul to mourn me when I die."

Thidiyan looked at the house, sighed thoughtfully and left.

After the drought was over and the rains came, Thidiyan got some cattle and began to graze them. He bought lands, and his children grew up. It was only then that Thidiyan's wife let her hair grow long. Every time she stroked her hair, she would smile to herself. In time, Thidiyan completely forgot about Siddu Reddiar, Nachiyar, and their family.

One day he saw a young man atop Mottaiparai on the hillock. His eyes looked familiar, like the eyes of someone he knew.

"Are you Thidiyan?" The young man asked, his face tense.

Thidiyan nodded.

"Do you know who I am?"

"Are you Nachiyaramma's son?" Thidiyan said, peering at his face.

He nodded, and pulling out the knife tucked at his waist, stabbed Thidiyan in the abdomen again and again.

"I have come to take some hair from your head and place it on my mother's grave. Only then will her soul rest in peace."

No one knew that it was Nachiyar who had chopped off Thidiyan's wife's hair, or that it was Nachiyar's son who was responsible for Thidiyan's death. Thidiyan, now dead, was deified, and till today, goats are sacrificed and feasts are offered in his memory.

As Poosari Muniyandi concluded narrating the story of Thidiyan, my mind was filled with wonder. When I returned after finishing my survey work, Muniyandi brought a box made of palm leaf and opened it for me.

There was a clump of hair folded and kept inside. Whose hair was it—Nachiyar's or Pooncholai's? No one knew. I asked the poosari and he replied,

"How does it matter whose it is? This is hair that was chopped off. It is bound to cause ruin, isn't it?" The poosari laughed.

I had to nod and say yes.

The Rain Diary

It had started raining. It was a holiday, so Sunanda was also at home, watching the dark clouds through the window. I rushed outside with the rain gauge to measure the rainfall. There was a small garden where Sunanda grew different kinds of flowers in pots. The rain descended heavily from the sky.

The only thing I had learned from Appa was to measure the rainfall whenever it rained. I had developed this habit only after marriage. I really do not know why I measure the rain, but I have developed an indescribable fascination for it.

For over forty years, Appa had recorded the rainfall in every place where he had worked. No one knew the reason for this. Even on the days that he was at home, he would place a vessel outside the house whenever it rained to measure the rainfall. No one had ever asked him why he did this.

Appa kept a record of the measurements in a notebook with a red leather cover. He had many such notebooks. He had never shown his rain ledgers to anyone.

Every human being has a habit that is inscrutable to the rest of the world, and this is something I learnt from Appa's habit of measuring the rain. He did not know that I too measure the rain like him. In fact, we had never even discussed the topic of rain. But for some odd reason, I wanted to emulate this particular habit of his. In every other way, I very scrupulously avoided being like Appa, but this is one habit that clung to me.

In the beginning, I would wonder what purpose it possibly served, measuring the rain. But now, as soon as the rain stops and I am about to find out the exact quantity of rainfall, in that moment, I feel my heart bursting with a strange joy. As soon as I record the numbers in my diary, my mind wants to check if there is a record of the same amount of rainfall on any other day in the past. If there were any such days, I would try to find out if there was anything in common between them. I discovered that there were some rare similarities between two different days with the same amount of rainfall. It was then that I realised my strange little habit was not just a game, it was a rare interest.

After I came to the USA, I strongly felt the changes in weather patterns. In Madurai where I had grown up, the contrast between seasons was not as stark. The summer was fierce, and the windy and rainy days were infrequent. There would be mild rain and mildly cool days—overall, it was warm all year round. There was nothing new in Madurai, everything, including the people, were remnants of the past. It was so long since the river Vaigai had floods that no one even remembered that the river existed. So I never witnessed rain that fell incessantly for days.

But life in America was different, as was the weather. Here the weather changed frequently, sometimes even over the course of a single day. The weather in the morning when you set out of the house would not be the same as when you reached your workplace. It is here that I first experienced fully the speed of the wind, the fierceness of the rain, the falling snow and the fragrance of the spring, and yet it is to rain that I remain partial.

In Seattle, in the evenings, rain like this is quite usual. The meteorological centre does forecast how long it will rain for, when it will stop and all that, but doesn't the mind rejoice the moment it sees rain?

The rain does something to me. I cannot express clearly just what it does to me, even though I have felt the rain and watched it so many times, for so many years. When we first came to this country, my wife Sunanda often told me, "The rain here is not like the rain at home."

"I don't see any difference," I would reply.

"No, Suku, I am afraid of this rain. There is something so masculine about it...it's a virile rain."

"Are you afraid because it falls forcefully?"

"No, I just don't like this rain. It is an intemperate rain."

Sunanda is always like this; with a few words, she can make you feel exactly what she is feeling. She is an avid reader, while I just scan the sports magazines. The rain I experienced in America was, like she said, an intemperate rain which could unnerve people. Even then, I liked the American rain.

I would sit watching the rain through the glass window some days, and other days I would be driving my car through the rain, enjoying the force of the falling lines of water. Every time it rained, deep in my heart I expected something to happen, for the rain to do something. Rain has the ability to upset our ordinary, everyday lives, but to what extent depends on its ferocity. Isn't that so?

Rain holds a secret within itself. I do not know what that secret is, but rain can make us feel that something unknown without the aid of words. Back home, I have often felt it.

One cannot...one mustn't watch the rain constantly or for very long, for if we do, the mind slips away and is no longer in our control. The mind like a plant surrenders itself slowly and completely to the rain. At times like that I feel as if the rain is pouring down on my head even though I am indoors, and that my heart is brimming.

Why is the rain so inscrutable?

Why is getting drenched so sensual, so joyful?

Isn't rain something that only happens outside of us?

Rain opens the eyes inside us that are closed—yes, our body awakens. But the body cannot conquer the rain, it is the rain that conquers the body, that weakens its barriers and urges us to search for another body...it arouses us. Rain is sorcery, it is a magic web, no...it is countless arms of water embracing the earth.

The rain does something to me, I feel so many things, my thoughts bubble up within me and I suddenly glow like an electric bulb with current surging through its filament.

I feel this way today too.

I ran out into the garden and fixed the rain gauge, staring at the rain with amazement as though I was seeing rainfall for the first time. Sunanda brought out a towel and asked me to come indoors and dry my hair. I took the towel from her but stood without drying myself, still dazed by the rain. She snatched it back from me and began rubbing my hair dry.

"You are like a frog! Your nature changes when it is about to rain...there is an extra happiness in you."

I pressed my face to the towel and spoke.

"Your nature too, it changes. You talk a lot more than usual on the days it rains. You behave, inexplicably, like a ten-year-old girl. I have noticed that."

Sunanda pulled the towel from my face and asked me, surprised, "Really? It's nothing of that sort. Maybe it is because I feel a sense of solitude more strongly in times of rain."

"That is the nature of rain, isn't it?"

"No, Suku, it is not the rain's nature to isolate anyone. Rather, it unites what lies separate. Rain is a big kiss that the world receives. Every drop kisses something, be it a tree, a plant, a rock or a roof... everything is kissed by the rain, and is truly kissed with love. I have sensed this myself," said Sunanda.

"Do you see how your way of speaking has changed?" I teased her. The rain had grown more intense, and Sunanda was looking out at the rain. I too watched the rain silently.

Sunanda broke the silence.

"When we were back home, I would wait for the rain. You know why? Because it was only when it rained that we could fully feel the warmth of the home, the closeness of people...even the nights seemed brighter. I loved to hear the sound of the falling rain as I slept. It sounded like sacred chants being uttered in a monotone. But ever since we have moved here, somehow I am just unable to become one with the rain. To tell you the truth, Suku, when it rains I always fear something unexpected is going to happen."

"What will happen? Why are you afraid?"

"I don't know. I can't clearly think of a reason why. But the fear is real. At times like this, even when I look at you, I feel as if I am alone with a total stranger."

"But I am a stranger, no? Aren't we tied together only by our marriage?"

"Most times I do not feel that way. It feels like we have known each other since childhood—I even imagine having seen you as a young boy. But when it starts to rain, I begin to feel that you are a stranger, a person I don't know at all. I try to rein in my mind, restrain these strange thoughts...or I run to the bedroom and lie down and close my eyes. Why, Suku, why does this happen?"

"Just the reverse happens to me, Sunanda. It is only when it rains that I feel the closest to you, and I feel such intense affection for you, my wife. You are here for me, you have come here only for my sake. You have come far away from the people you love, your home, your dreams...everything. So I feel I must keep you happy. When it is raining and I kiss you, it is like kissing an infant. You become so soft, so weightless...like foam."

"Now you too have begun talking like me, Suku." She affectionately petted me.

The trees outside were swaying to and fro, unable to bear the lashing of the rain and the wind. A streak of lightning cut through the sky.

"How about some coffee?" I asked.

"If you make it."

"Men feel hungrier on rainy days."

"Then you make something for us to eat," she said, leaning back on the sofa.

It is only on some rare days that Sunanda would ask me like this, and on those days I too love to cook. At other times, even if I offer to help in the kitchen, she won't let me. She would say that it was enough if I helped with the household chores.

I made an unidentifiable hodgepodge, an upma-like dish, with bread, onions and eggs. It continued to rain. The rain opens hidden doors in our hearts. All of this would have never happened in summer.

I carried the hot coffee and upma to her.

"It tastes different when men cook," she observed as she ate.

"It tastes good because of the ambience, the rain outside. And because it is hot and fresh, that is all there is to it."

"Would your parents ever talk to each other about the rain like this?" she asked with a smile.

I shook my head.

"My parents spoke very little to each other. Appa was a railway station master. The years of his service, he spent half the time in Kerala and the other half in Tamil Nadu. He never took us to stay with him in the railway quarters. He always lived alone. We lived in Appa's ancestral house in Madurai. He would come home on the weekends—I wondered why he bothered. Anyway, it was Amma who ran the house, educated us, took us to the hospital when we were sick and stayed up all night with us. Appa only gave us money every month."

"Did your Appa ever beat your Amma?"

"I don't have any such memory. Appa never got angry with anyone. He spoke very little. When I told him I had cracked the engineering entrance and was offered a seat, for the first time Appa indicated his happiness by saying 'Santhosham'. That single word was all he expressed. He did not visit me even once at the hostel. After the first meeting arranged by our parents to see if you and I liked each other, he asked me if I liked you. That was all the concern he showed."

"Do you hate your father?"

"No, I don't, but I wonder why he behaved like that. Mostly I think of him only as some man we knew...I am unable to fit him into the image of a father."

Sunanda seemed to be lost in deep thought. Then sipping her coffee, she said,

"My father was totally the opposite of yours. He insisted on having an elaborate spread for every meal. He would not wash even a hanky. Everything had to be done as per his wishes, from the children's homework to lighting the lamp before the deity. What was purchased was always his selection, be it a coconut or a silk saree. We would yearn for him to go away somewhere for a few days. Even when he went out, he would be back home by night. There was no respite at all for Amma. He would be bad-mouthing someone or the other all day. He had no taste or interest in anything. He was never sensitive to another's pain. The house was his kingdom, he was the uncrowned emperor, and we were his servants."

"Wasn't it difficult?" I asked.

"None of us had to face it alone, so we all got used to it."

"Why are we discussing our fathers today? Is it the rain that made us do it?" I asked.

"At least the rain reminded us of them."

She spoke the truth. The rain unearths memories that have been buried deep. The heart lets out a deep sigh inside us. We cannot articulate the reason for that sigh.

"The rain reminds us of so many things."

"Including the fact that we have no children?"

"Not at all," I said.

"As soon as it starts to rain, the thought that we have no children starts to bother me."

"Why do you think like that?"

"There is a lot of guilt in me, Suku. Have you ever considered that I might be the cause for our childlessness?"

"You are not the cause. Let us not talk about this now."

"No, it is when it rains that we must discuss unwelcome subjects. Words seem less hurtful when it rains, and we can talk freely without hurting each other."

"Why bring this up now?"

"Do you feel sorry that we have no children?"

"I do want children. But I don't think about it all the time and feel sad."

"Both of us are healthy, we enjoy having sex with each other, and yet we have no child. Why, Suku?"

"Only the doctors would be able to tell us why."

"The doctor said that we are both healthy physically, but empty inside. He asked us to set that right. Do you think it is the emptiness that is the cause?"

"Nothing of that sort. I think we are very happy," I said.

"Look at the rain and tell me if we are happy."

"We *are* happy."

"We are sad too."

"It is not wrong to feel sad."

"Don't you ever wonder who or what is the cause for this sadness?"

"If we do that, we will needlessly imagine things."

"The truth is it is only our bodies that come together and unite. The mind is not aroused. When stone rubs against stone, sparks fly and a fire is born on its own. But in our relationship, we are like two smooth pebbles rubbing against each other."

"I do not analyse what happens in bed."

"I too was like that, Suku. But now I have allowed unnecessary thoughts to grow. I don't like myself anymore. And this reminds me of my inabilities even more. The rain troubles me. I feel as if it is announcing to the world that I am the cause."

"This is all your imagination. You are just thinking too much."

"No, Suku. Something has really happened to me. I don't know how to tell you. I am unable to bear it."

"Let us not talk about this now, Sunanda. I don't like it," I said sharply.

"At some point or the other, we have to, no?"

"Why should we? Is life only about having children? Is there nothing else?"

"But I want children. And I am unable to have a child. It *is* a problem, an unsolvable problem."

"There is no problem. We will surely have children one day."

"That is what I have been thinking for the last six years. I have not been able to speak about this with anyone till now. Suddenly I feel like talking about it today, so let us talk, Suku."

"What are you going to achieve by talking?"

"Some kind of solace, maybe?"

"Why are you talking like this Sunanda? You alone are important to me. Children may happen, but even if they don't happen, it does not matter."

"Can we be like this forever? What will happen when we are old?"

"I never think about our old age. That is too far away to even imagine. I am only thirty-six now."

"You don't understand me, Suku." She started to cry.

I put my arms around her shoulder to comfort her. She curled up on the sofa and began sobbing profusely.

It was raining again. The evening had darkened into night. The water from above dissolved and washed away the light in the sky.

I wondered if I should go and stand outside.

One cannot comprehend the rain merely by getting wet. One must internalise it fully, and for that, getting drenched is of no use.

Sunanda's sobs were slowly subsiding.

I put on some music, a violin sonata by Schubert. Schubert is a composer I like. I always keep CDs of his music in my car because his music is my only companion when I travel long distances. It is only after I came to this country that I started listening to Beethoven, Mozart, Vivaldi and Wagner, and how they have grown on me!

The music filled our house. Sunanda had calmed down by now, she was no longer crying. I went and sat near her and slowly stroked her forehead. She held my hand tight and said, "Sorry."

"Are you feeling cold, Sunanda?"

"What shall I cook tonight?"

"Make something easy."

"I want to cook a big meal. When I feel very happy or very sad, I like to cook a lot."

"As you wish. Just tell me what I should do."

"Come to the kitchen and tell me a story."

"Story? But I don't know any."

"Try to remember one...perhaps a tale heard long ago but forgotten. I want to hear a story."

"I'll try, let me see if I can remember any. Look, the rain has almost stopped."

Sunanda went to wash her face. I could hear her opening the door of the refrigerator, taking out the vegetables and then washing them. I stood looking out at the rain through the glass window.

Sunanda was singing, her voice floated out from the kitchen: "*Kannan ennum mannan perai solla solla*". It was the song from the movie *Vennira Aadai*.

Sunanda liked this song very much, and I liked hearing her sing. I wanted to sing along with her, but inhibition stopped me. I turned off the Schubert so that I could hear her better.

She was lost in herself, singing aloud. The rain was losing its force and would stop in a few minutes.

I did not know yet how much it had rained today. I racked my brain for a story to tell Sunanda. I could not think of a single one, except for the fox and the crow fables.

Then a story came to mind. When we had management training in the office, I had heard someone narrate it.

I decided I would tell her that one and went close to her. The aroma of her cooking wafted through the house.

"Ready for a story?" I asked her.

"Tell me a story about me."

"About you? What kind of story?"

"Something...anything."

"Okay. All of a sudden, you, your body, it turns into ice. You become a snow angel. To turn you back into a woman again, I cross seven seas and seven mountains and kill an ogre. And then I bring you back. How do you like the story?"

"I want to remain a snow angel! Come, feel my hands."

They were cold.

"You too should turn into snow," she said.

"Today you are speaking and acting very strangely."

The rain had stopped.

"What does your rain gauge say?" she asked me.

I went to the garden and checked. It showed 109 mm of rain. I flipped through the pages of my rain record to check the other dates when it had rained the same amount. There were five other days.

It suddenly occurred to me: why not send an email to Appa about this rain? Ever since he retired, Appa had been housebound with only the computer for company. And after Amma died, it was my sister's family that took care of him. Whenever I went home, I asked Appa repeatedly to visit us here, but he always refused.

The food was more delicious than the meals Sunanda usually cooked. We polished off everything, and Sunanda commented that it was because both of us had been very hungry. Then we decided to watch a movie. We chose *Springtime in a Small Town*. As we were watching the movie, Sunanda snuggled close and kissed me, a long, passionate kiss. Like a wave, lust washed over us. We laughed without reason all night.

Next morning, I sent an email to Appa before I left for office. I mentioned the amount of rain the previous night, and wrote that like him, I too measure the rain.

In the evening when I returned home, I saw Appa's reply.

> I am happy that you measure the rain too. Sixteen times I have recorded rain that had the same measurement. The details of those days are attached. Let at least the rain bring us close.

Sunanda read the mail too.

"There is some train of thought that runs through your Appa's mind, which is why he records the rain. You try to find out," Sunanda said.

"It is indeed wonderful that the rain is bringing us together."

"I can never forget last night's rain," she said, smiling.

Work took me out of town for the next five days. Sunanda told me that Appa had called. She had not asked why.

I sat before the computer intending to write him a long mail.

> Appa,
>
> I had never been fond of you. I have never felt that you were fond of me. But now I keep thinking of you often. I feel that you hold a mystery within you.
>
> When you worked in the railways, you did not take us to see new places by train often. Family for you was a place of rest, an evidence of your manhood.

But you have never scolded us, you have never complained to us about your work, you never shared anything about your health or your income.

You are an extremely stubborn man.

Appa, even old age has not changed you. You are still so resolute. I do not know how or why you developed this habit of measuring rain. But because of this you have created for me an image of a very different person, unique even. It is this image that draws me to you now.

I was always very careful not to become like you. So I would compare even a small act of mine with yours. But suddenly one day I began to measure the rain, just like you. I did it secretly till yesterday. I am unable to articulate this, but the rain helps me comprehend many things. When I saw the details of the similar rains you have recorded, I felt as if you have met the siblings of yesterday's rain.

I really want to read your rain diary. Can you send it by post, please?

Yours,

Your son

I sent the email and sat staring at the empty screen of my computer. I wondered what Appa's face would look like when he reads this. But try as I might, I could not recall his face at all.

That night in bed, Sunanda asked me, "Why don't you ask your father to come and stay with us?"

"He won't come." I turned over.

"Your father's voice is just like yours. I could not tell the difference over phone." Sunanda stroked my hair as she said this.

I did not say anything. I was thinking of the details of the rain that he had sent.

Appa sent an email that same night...a slightly longer letter.

Dear Sukumar,

You should not try to give meaning to the rain. Leave it be. That is how I lived my life. The rain alone was my teacher. It is one huge drop that shatters and falls as rain. The one who learns to look at the rain will not be shaken by anything. Sorrow would not be able to do anything to him. That is how I learnt to overcome my loneliness.

It is not easy to spend one's nights in a railway station, all alone, with no other human being in sight. At times like those, the rain has comforted me. I surrendered myself to the rain. You and I, we are two tiny witnesses to the long journey of the eternal rain. I have one view of the rain, you see another. Measure the rain. Then you will not only begin to understand the rain, but also yourself.

When you come here on your next visit, I will not be alive. My rain record is not for others to read, they are mine alone. Let them die with me. However heavy a rainfall there may be, who is going to remember it?

I will leave one thing for you. It is the rain gauge that I used. Give it to my grandson or granddaughter as my gift if they ever ask you. That single joy alone I beg of you.

And I will tell you one secret. I was attached to another woman besides your mother. I met her in Kerala when I worked there. I married her too. She has two sons. This was known to your mother. That is why I did not stay much in the house with you all. Your mother was a wonderful woman, I did not deserve her. I tried to dissolve my mistakes and my guilt in the rain, hoping it would wash it all away. But I could not. What could the rain do?

Women alone can hear the rain's secrets, men cannot. The rain alone can make this world come alive, just as women do.

My love and blessings to your wife.

Your Appa

I was shocked when I read this. None of us had an inkling that Appa had another family. How did Amma accept this? Why did she not get furious? Why did Amma forgive Appa's weaknesses? I felt angry with Amma.

I asked Sunanda to read the email.

"Your mother had told me about this. It was I who did not tell you."

"Why?"

"There are many things that we just have to accept, we have no choice. Isn't that what the rain here teaches us?"

I kept looking at Sunanda silently. I understood that in her words lay a deep truth.

The Pigeons Flew into His Soul

It was sheer chance that Govardhan saw those pigeons when he leaned against the window of his office on the first floor. Facing his office was the Food Corporation godown. The compound had very high walls. The pigeons sat in a row on top of the black walls.

How many are there? he wondered. He counted, there were sixteen. The office had changed Govardhan. If he had seen these pigeons in his younger days, he would not have counted them. Then he would have drowned himself in fanciful thoughts of the birds as messengers between lovers. But an office clerk who was barely three years away from retirement can hardly go on such flights of fancy, can he? So he just counted them.

In truth, a person who has been in government service for over thirty years acquires the qualities of a government office. Unbeknownst to them, their face, body and actions are slowly transformed and increasingly come to resemble those old government office desks.

Moreover, someone who spends the entire day, from the time he enters the office till he leaves, adding, subtracting, totalling and checking accounts, won't he feel like counting whatever he saw?

Govardhan's children would tease him. When they went out to eat, he would have calculated the amount in his mind before the bill came.

"Appa, why are you telling us how much? Anyway the computer will print out the bill, won't it?" When his daughter asked him this, he had no answer.

It was not just a habit, it was also his upbringing. He belonged to the generation which had been taught to count every paisa spent and to keep accounts meticulously. But nowadays who maintains accounts? Back in those days, how many times had Amma scolded him for losing a five paisa coin at the provision store? Is it like that today? No, paisas do not matter, nor do rupees.

But those trained in the old ways cannot change. So nowadays when Govardhan and his family went out to eat, he calculated the total, but kept it to himself.

The thought that he was going to start a new life in Chennai after he finished his college had brought him such joy. But these thirty-one years in Chennai had not been particularly memorable. He had bought a house and the children had completed their education...that was all.

None of the places where he had been transferred to for work—Chidambaram, Cuddalore, Karur or Rasipuram—resonated in his heart. He was a miniscule part of the city where more than a crore lived. An insignificant, unidentifiable particle. Can you distinguish between one drop and another in a torrential downpour?

When he got a job in Chennai, he took a room on rent and stayed there. He did not go straight back to his room when he left office. Instead, he went roaming around the city—the temple, the beach, the Triplicane lanes, political gatherings, libraries, lectures, concerts, the shops at night...time just slipped by unnoticed.

The room of the mansion where he stayed had no facilities, but he did not mind that. Sometimes on Sundays he would even end up watching three movies back to back. He went in search of Bilal

Biryani at night. Then one day everything palled. He got married and found a separate house to stay in with his new bride, and somehow the city shrank.

Even going to the beach became a tiresome thing. Once at the beach, he felt as if thousands of people were screaming and he thought he would suffocate. When his daughter dragged him to the edge of the water because she wanted to feel the waves on her feet, a huge fear overcame him.

What if the waves drag me away?

Not only did he not go close to the waves himself, he stopped his daughter too.

"You are getting old, that is why you are afraid of everything," his wife chided him.

It was true, he realised. Was this really a needless fear? When one grows old, why do the littlest of things assume mammoth proportions? Anxiety and fear seem to build up to the point of exploding. One day he was speaking about this with the office typist, Sundari.

"Our mind feels unsettled when our body refuses to listen to us. Then we keep thinking about our body all day. Who worried about health at twenty? We even chewed on iron and walked on. But now? It takes half a day to digest one *vadai*," Sundari grumbled.

Everyone laughed on hearing this. But Govardhan felt sad. What she said was true. At the root of all fear was this body. In truth, we ourselves ruin our bodies. And this government office played an important role in that devastation. What is the point in worrying now? It was boring to see each day pass by in this big city.

Nothing could hold his interest...films, newspapers, temples, music...everything seemed dull. Earlier his friends played carrom in the office, and they would sip tea and chat for hours on end. All that came to an end with the coming of the cellphone. Playing, laughing, chatting—everything came to an end, and those ties of friendship were severed.

Govardhan felt that he was doing a thankless job as he came to work every day. When he placed his lunch box on the floor and pulled out the desk drawer, he felt as though he was really very old. As if cobwebs spread not just over his office but over him too, and they could not be swept away. He thought of himself as a man covered with cobwebs.

It was on a day like this, oppressed by ennui, anxiety and emptiness, that Govardhan began to watch the pigeons. After five minutes, he began to really notice the whiteness of the pigeons. How white! How pure! No dust or smoke could change this whiteness.

The pigeons sat in a row, as if they were waiting for something. Who was the steno among them? Who was the head clerk? There are no such distinctions among the pigeons. One preened its feathers, another looked ready to take flight, and two were rubbing their beaks against each other. One pigeon sat a little away from the rest. Maybe it was also fed up with the city like him.

Govardhan kept looking at the pigeons. Suddenly all of them flew away. Where were they going? Where did they live? Why this sudden haste?

The bare compound wall without the pigeons resembled a government office on a holiday. For a long time he stood there staring at the wall.

"Sir, what are you looking at on the godown wall?" One of the head clerks, Arunan, turned around and asked him.

"Nothing. It was stuffy inside," he lied.

That evening, the pigeons occupied his mind until he returned home. Strangely, he picked up a pencil and started drawing a pigeon in an old diary. His wife thought he was doing some office work. He, however, could not draw the bird as he had imagined. He tried four or five times but failed.

Next morning, as soon as he had reached the office, he eagerly looked for the pigeons. They were not there. He kept looking every now and then till it was afternoon. Around three o'clock, one by one, they came and sat on the wall. The same sixteen pigeons. They sat together like inseparable friends.

He first thought they came only to peck at the grains. But when he looked carefully it was evident that they were not eating anything. Then what were they doing? Why did they congregate there?

Suddenly they took off, flew in a circle a few times and then alighted on the wall as before. Was this wall their playground? Or their meditation hall? Who was the oldest among them? Which town did they belong to? It was not possible for Govardhan to guess. But watching them was enticing. For a long time, he leaned on the chair and watched them.

"Earlier, more pigeons used to come, sir. Now there are fewer," commented Sundaram, another head clerk, standing behind him.

"Have you watched them?" Govardhan asked.

"I look at them sometimes, just like that. What else can one do to pass time in this office?" Sundaram replied, rubbing some Amrutanjan on his forehead.

"Do the pigeons sit only on this wall? Or are there other places too where they sit?"

"You will find many pigeons in front of the mosque, and even opposite the old Safire theatre. But not near the American embassy though, perhaps even the pigeons are terrified of the embassy and have flown away." Sundaram laughed.

Why did they always come in the same numbers? How did this affinity develop? Was this just a habit? Why did the pigeons keep flying around in this metropolis instead of going away to the wilds?

He wanted to get out of the office and see the pigeons up close. He slipped into his chappals and climbed down.

The watchman was not to be seen at the gate. The place was filled with dried grass and nameless plants. As he walked closer, he caught the thick smell of paddy being steamed. There was a torn poster on the wall blackened by rainwater that had dripped down.

Govardhan went near the wall where the pigeons sat. He hid himself fearing they might fly away if they heard his footsteps. One of the pigeons saw him but turned away as though it had not. He could hear the cooing of the pigeons clearly from where he stood. It was like an asthma patient wheezing. The birds started to take off as though their time was up. They flew past him. The single pigeon that sat at a distance away from the rest flew away as well.

When he walked back to his office, the watchman asked him, "Whom did you want to see, sir?"

"Just the next office," he lied with a smile.

The watchman did not ask any further questions.

What is this madness? Why did I come down to see the pigeons? he asked himself. Even after he was back in his office, his thoughts kept circling around the pigeons.

That day he did not go home straight from office but began to look for other places where pigeons could be spotted. It was amusing. But contrary to what he thought, they could be seen in many places. He decided to start counting them. His heart was inexplicably filled with joy.

He began to look for pigeons in all the places he passed on his way home—Triplicane, Mylapore, T. Nagar, Saidapettai, West Mambalam, Chromepet, Tambaram and so on. His heart overflowed with happiness to find out where all they gathered, how many of them, what they looked like, and more.

He got a small pocket book to note down these details. Suddenly the city had transformed for him and he felt that it held within itself many undiscovered secrets. For some reason, no one's attention was drawn to the fact that there were so many pigeons in the city, thousands of them.

Why did the pigeons live in such constrained spaces? Were they ascetics? Why did they not squabble noisily? Why were they mainly found near mosques, temples and churches? Was it perhaps because they were messengers from the heavens? The more he looked at them, the more he felt that the pigeon was a fascinating bird.

He started to browse TV channels to see if any of them featured pigeons. He was always looking at images of pigeons on the internet. Neither his children nor his wife could comprehend this sudden change in him.

He began pigeon-watching on Sundays too. It is said that once pigeons find a mate they do not separate. Govardhan felt it must be true. He was amazed when he found out that pet pigeons came back home no matter where you left them.

Were the pigeons like him? Was their home their whole universe? Why did they love their cage so much? The sky is so vast, they can easily fly away, can't they?

The watchman of the Food Corporation godown said that even if the wall on which they perched was knocked down, they would still come to the same spot. Isn't that foolishness? Or have the pigeons realised that the walls are not mere perches?

After he was caught by this pigeon madness, he travelled by electric train for a few days and then by bus for another few, all the while noting the pigeons on these different routes. He also took the share-auto sometimes, and on one such auto ride to Royapettah, he met a purdah-clad young woman squeezed between co-passengers who leaned out to see the pigeons sitting on a tin roof. He was amused.

The share-auto passengers were irritated by her behaviour and ticked her off. She was not bothered however. She just laughed, and then offered an explanation on her own.

"I really love pigeons. We used to have pigeons at home. My Vappa used to take part in pigeon races."

Govardhan was intrigued by her remark about pigeons and her father.

The share-auto kept moving on its way. When it turned a curve, Govardhan pointed out, "On your left, there will be a mechanic shop. Keep an eye out, you will see pigeons there."

Like he had said, there was a group of pigeons in that spot. She started counting them hastily. Just as she finished counting, he said the right number.

"How did you know that they would be here?"

The twenty-something girl's sense of child-like wonder surprised him.

"I have noted down the details of all the flocks of pigeons in this city," he said, and showed her the small pocket notebook.

She could not believe it.

He handed over the notebook to her. She leafed through the pages quickly. The number of pigeons was recorded location-wise.

"Why do you count the pigeons?" she asked with a smile.

"Just like that, for no reason," he said, smiling back at her.

"I too would like to do that. But my husband does not like all this." She gently stroked the notebook.

When the share-auto stopped near the bridge, she returned his notebook and got down. Then she said, "You must not follow the pigeons. If you do, they will appear in your dreams."

Her remark made him happy. He yearned for a pigeon to appear in his dream...at least one pigeon. But he never had dreams. Sometimes in office he would daydream, but he never dreamed at night.

Until he reached home, he kept thinking of the girl and the pigeons. He went off to sleep by nine that night.

But he had no pigeon dreams.

However, a newfound happiness permeated his life. In the morning, as he shaved, he wondered if he would come across the girl in purdah that day. Suddenly he wanted to wear white like the pigeons. He started speaking softly and stopped shouting in anger. He had noticed that an unseen discipline ruled the pigeons. They do not wait for a command, and yet they all take flight together, suddenly, at the same time. They do not proclaim their hunger by cawing like the crows. These qualities of pigeons opened a door for him to experience the city anew.

A city is not meant for people alone. Thousands of pigeons and other birds, dogs, cats, rats, bacteria and much else live together. Each has its own hunger, its own search for food. No one gets anything easily. There is no sense of permanence in a city. One tries to find for oneself a place to perch...one has to.

Slowly his fear of life was beginning to recede.

Once on a Sunday, when he was roaming around the Royapettah clock tower looking for pigeons, he heard a voice calling from behind.

"I was the first to spot them."

It was the same young purdah-clad woman. She held a basket. He smiled at her in response.

"Is your house here, sir?"

"No, East Tambaram."

"You have come this far in search of pigeons?" Her tone mocked him.

"It's not like that. Today is a holiday, so I came this way," he parried.

"My Vappa was also like you, always thinking of pigeons. He used to talk to them. Do you?"

"No...I don't know."

"Vappa said that if we talk to pigeons, they will talk back to us."

"It must be true, then."

"Do you really trust me so much?"

Govardhan kept quiet, not knowing what to say.

"Will you give me that notebook?" she asked him.

"What will you give me in return?"

The young woman said she would buy him a cup of tea.

"Really?"

"Sure, but you must give me that notebook."

"What will you do with it?"

"I will keep it with me. And when I am sitting at home, I will imagine the places you have mentioned in it. You have written in detail about the places and the number of pigeons in each spot, have you not?"

"Won't you feel like going and seeing them in person?"

"Am I a man that I can keep following pigeons? Don't I have work to do?"

She must have felt that he would misunderstand her and think that she was referring to him.

"I didn't mean you." She laughed.

"But it is the truth."

"Aren't you angry?"

He shook his head.

She then invited him to a tea stall nearby and got him a cup of tea.

"Aren't you having tea?" he asked her.

"Ayyo! If people got to know I was standing by the road and having tea, they would surely kill me off."

Govardhan looked at her as he slowly sipped the tea. Her hands stretched out for the notebook.

"I won't give it."

"You cheated me?" she asked sadly.

"No, no. I was just teasing you. Here." He gave the notebook to her.

She put it in her basket without even opening it.

"What is your name?" he asked her.

She crossed the road and left without telling him. He stood there at the tea stall for a long time. He felt a strange mixture of joy and sadness in his heart.

That day he took the last bus home. He could not sleep. He got up and sat on the easy chair. As he leaned back, thoughts of that woman floated in his head.

Now she will be at home, with the notebook in hand, imagining the pigeons.

The city is strange in its ways...you never know when and how it brings two people together or why it separates them.

Suddenly he felt he had become twenty-five once more. He took out the old black-and-white photographs from his cupboard and looked at them. *This young man is not me. I have come a long way since those photographs*. He did not like the face he had at present.

He fell asleep on the easy chair thinking of her. Then a pigeon came in his dream.

Since then, he recalled the young woman every time he saw pigeons. Unconsciously, a sense of guilt began to creep in whenever he counted pigeons. He wondered if his wife would be able to detect that. Then he told himself that it was just a meeting, and nothing more.

Whenever he thought of the young woman in purdah, he felt as if a pigeon came to him, sat on his shoulder and then flew away.

He was a stone wall. Pigeons do not come to perch on the walls because the walls desire it. No, it is rather the wall that acquires a certain kind of beauty because the pigeons sit there. *This wall would have to continue thinking of the pigeon with great regret in its heart*, he thought.

One of the head clerks was talking to someone nearby in a loud voice, loud enough for Govardhan to overhear.

"Are men here only to eat and sleep, sir? Doesn't he need something for himself, something to rejoice? What is there, sir, in this city? It is all about money, money, money! It is like that at home, and in the city too it's just the same."

"Correct!" Govardhan said very loudly.

The head clerk turned and looked at him, puzzled.

Why did he say it so loudly?

Govardhan ducked to avoid the clerk's glance.

At that moment, it bothered him that the window near his seat was wide open.

The Price of an Angel's Wings

"Where is Appa?" Saranya asked the moment she woke up. Raghu heard her voice; he was checking his office accounts on his laptop.

Saranya came in pushing the door.

"Will the shop be open now, Appa?"

"No, dear. They will open only after ten."

"I'll bathe and get ready. We will go early."

"It's only seven now. What is the hurry? Take it easy."

Saranya's face fell. She stood there holding the door.

"Okay. We get ready, and then we will go," Raghu said.

Nodding her head happily, Saranya went towards the kitchen. Her school was going to celebrate the School Day, and she was taking part in a play. She needed an angel's costume and wings.

Renu herself had stitched the all-white costume for Saranya in two days. They just had to get the wings now. All night they searched online to find out where angel wings would be available. They needed large wings. Saranya firmly said that only then she would be able to hide her face in the wings while dancing.

All kinds of things were advertised on the internet, but not wings. Then Renu found a picture in one of her magazines of a

Russian girl dressed as an angel and showed it to them. It would be nice if they got glass wings like that, she said.

Where does one go looking for wings like that? Is there a shop in this big city that sells wings?

Raghu called his friend Kannan who works in movies.

"You'll get it in Sekar Cine Properties. It is near the Vadapalani Sivan temple. Go ask there," Kannan said.

Raghu asked him to forward the name of the shop and the phone number. In a few minutes he received the details on his phone. Raghu called the shop. But the phone kept ringing, there was no response. It was nine at night. Maybe the phone was out of order, he thought, so he searched on the internet using the name and address. But nothing came up.

With some impatience, he decided he would try just one last time.

"Sekar Properties," an old, raspy voice answered.

"Do you have wings?"

"Wings as in?"

"You know...what angels have...with feathers on them? My daughter is acting in a school play..." Raghu mumbled, trying to explain.

"We have them. What size do you want?"

"Large."

"You want to buy or hire?"

"For hire." Raghu thought it did not make sense to buy them for just a day's show.

"The cost depends on size. There are many in the godown. You can come and have a look."

"When can I come?"

"Come after ten in the morning. I'll ask someone to show them to you."

"Your name?" Before Raghu could finish his question, the call disconnected.

Saranya was very enthusiastic when he shared the information with her.

"We'll buy it, Appa. Then I can use it for my birthday too."

"Let us see, sweetie."

"How much do the wings cost, Appa?"

"I didn't ask. They told us to come and see in person."

"Where is the shop, Appa?"

"In Vadapalani."

"Is it near the temple we always go to?"

"Near that, yes."

"How long will it take for us to go there from home?"

"Half an hour."

"Tomorrow is Sunday. Will the shop be open?" Renu interjected.

"I asked the old man, he told us to come. Is it a government office that it will be closed on Sundays?" Raghu was getting annoyed now.

"Rani lives near the Vadapalani temple. If possible, let's go get a *murukku*-maker from her."

"We will see," Raghu said half-heartedly.

Saranya spread her arms wide and began dancing. In her mind she was wearing the wings they were going to buy the next day.

Saranya was in the fourth standard in school. Raghu would tell her fairy tales at bedtime. Even when she felt sleepy, she would force herself to keep her eyes open and continue to listen to the stories. Raghu, who used to be very enthusiastic in the beginning, slowly lost interest and just listlessly narrated the stories now.

When she listened to these stories, Saranya would enter a fantasy world. She constantly asked questions. Sometimes, Raghu would feel irritated and ask her to shut up and listen.

Two years ago for the Independence Day programme in her school, Saranya was chosen to be a part of a Rajasthani group dance. She wore a colourful costume, complete with earrings, necklace and bangles worn by the women of the desert region, had make up on and danced with great gusto. Raghu and Renu went to see the school programme. The chief guest went on and on giving a totally unrelated speech about world economy. After thirteen items, when Saranya's Rajasthani dance commenced, they were extremely tired. The dance lasted three minutes. Placed in the second row, Saranya was a small dot moving around.

All the students who danced on that occasion got mementoes. It was a small cup the size of a finger. Saranya would hug it to sleep as if it was a big trophy. The teacher who had trained her then was the one who had selected her to be an angel for the upcoming performance.

When Saranya first told her parents about this, Renu's reaction was sharp.

"Waste of money!"

Saranya cried at her mother's comment. Raghu consoled her.

"You will act. I will get you the costume." He cheered her up.

Mother and daughter went around making enquiries, trying to see if an angel's costume would be readily available. In the end, Renu decided to stitch it herself. She bought some material and stitched a frock with a lot of frills. Saranya's joy knew no bounds when she first tried it on.

She took a selfie of herself. She went around in the same costume all morning, refusing to take it off. Raghu thought that Saranya had a new glow about her and looked lovely in the angel's dress. He took a photo holding his daughter's hand.

"If we buy large wings and fix them to my back, it will be super, Appa. Then we will take a picture, frame it and hang it on the wall here," Saranya suggested.

It sounded like a good idea. Children obviously see no difference between the real and the imaginary. Saranya had begun to think she really was an angel. Some days she sat at the window staring at the sky, imagining how it would be if she flew away. She shook her empty hands and looked down to see if stars dropped from her palms. Sometimes she looked at the birds with wonder.

One day she asked Renu wistfully.

"Amma, why don't we all have wings?"

"Not just us—even lions, tigers and elephants do not have wings."

"It would be nice if we do..."

"We don't have to pay for the school van then. We would fly to school."

Saranya seemed not to pay much heed to her mother, and kept imagining what it would be like if she could fly to school. Then she laughed to herself and asked, "Does any bird have four wings?"

"Don't be stupid," Renu shut her up.

After that Saranya would not ask Renu anything. She spoke to herself, asked herself questions, and was happy to be in the world of her own imagination.

Raghu was riding his scooter. Saranya rode pillion and looked at everyone passing by. There was heavy traffic on the road. At the Porur junction stood a group of policemen. Saranya was afraid.

"How much further, Appa?" she asked, eyeing the police.

Raghu did not reply.

When they reached Sekar Cine Properties, it was open. A man was reading the paper. A broken palanquin was kept outside the shop. Saranya stood looking at it with curiosity. Raghu climbed up the steps.

"Sir," he called to draw the man's attention. The man lowered the paper and looked at Raghu.

"They came and took all the crowns away."

Raghu was bewildered.

"You are one of the TV serial people, right?" the man asked, puzzled.

"No."

"Sorry, sir. Minerva Creations said they will send someone. I thought it was you."

"No. I had called last night. An elderly person had answered."

"Oh, Tilakar? He is the clerk, sir. What do you want? Are you making a short film?"

"No, I want two angel's wings. My daughter is acting in a school play."

The man looked at Saranya standing alone and said to Raghu, "Pappa has grown very thin, hasn't she?"

Raghu nodded as if to say yes.

"Which school?" The man asked Saranya directly.

She answered in a soft voice.

"Do you want an angel's dress or just the wings?"

"Just the wings," Raghu said.

"It is in the godown, sir. The shop boy has gone to buy food. As soon as he returns, I will send him with you."

"How much will it cost?"

"For a small size, the rent is 250 per day, if it is medium, it is 350, and for large it will be 800, sir."

"Do you have wings made of glass?" Raghu asked.

"If you want I can make it with fibreglass. It will cost 2000."

Saranya was looking wide-eyed at the old record player, the wooden horse, china vases, cardboard daggers and other curios that were stored there. A boy, about fifteen years old, arrived on a cycle. From the handle bar hung an old flask and a food parcel in a plastic bag. He saw Raghu and Saranya and frowned.

"Anna, *vadakari* was not available. So I bought just *idli*," he told the man.

"These people want wings. Take them to the godown."

The boy picked up a bunch of keys and told Raghu, "Come with me, sir. The godown is in the next street."

Saranya and Raghu followed him. A cow was pulling at a poster torn and hanging from the wall, and chewing on it. Feathers from a hen floated around in the air. Someone had left his cycle parked right across the street. A boy was eating puffs outside a bakery shop sitting on his cycle. A tricycle push-cart, unable to enter the street, made a huge racket.

The godown was in an ancient building. The boy opened the door and went in.

"What is your name, Appa?" Raghu asked.

"Palani."

All kinds of old things were piled up inside the house. There were very many clocks, old paintings, a picture of Gandhi and some group photos hanging on the wall. There were swords, shields, crowns and thrones needed for historical movies. There were stuffed birds, chairs large and small, porcelain sculptures, different kinds of guns and rifles, flower vases, life-size mirrors, serial lights, turbans in red and green, a variety of wine glasses, old radios, backdrops for plays and so on. Raghu was amazed looking at them.

Palani opened another door inside.

"See, sir," he said.

Inside the room, wings of different types and sizes were arranged on the wall. How many different kinds there must have been? Why would they have made them? Saranya in all eagerness looked on. Raghu bent down to pick up a pair of wings. It was made of transparent paper, and had an elastic so it could be tied on to the waist. He called Saranya close and fixed the wings. She went all shy.

"Is it bumping against your elbows?"

"No, Appa."

He removed it and fixed another pair. She took pictures with the different sets of wings one by one with great enthusiasm. Finally they found a large pair, just like she wanted. Palani said that embedded in the wings were small lights which would flicker when the arms attached to the wings moved. Saranya liked this pair the best.

"We'll buy this one, Appa."

"How much is it?"

"Do you want to buy?" Palani asked.

"No, for hire."

"Thousand rupees per day, sir."

"But the owner said eight hundred."

"Those are without the lights."

"The price is too high," Raghu said.

"Talk to the owner, sir. If it is hired for a day, it must be returned by eight the next morning. Otherwise the rate doubles."

"Don't worry, I will return them promptly."

Saranya stood holding the wings in her hand, brimming with joy.

They locked up the godown and walked back. Saranya held on to the wings tightly as she walked. A crow sitting on the tree seemed to be mocking her, but for Saranya, it was a matter of great pride to walk with the wings.

At the shop, the owner looked at the wings and quoted the price.

"It will cost one thousand, sir. This is export material," he said.

"Please, that is too much. It is just for a school programme," Raghu tried to bargain.

"These days every school takes fees in the range of thirty to forty thousand. Do any of you bargain with them? Here too, it is one flat rate."

Raghu was annoyed by the owner's tone, but he suppressed his anger and tried again.

"So, what do you say, what price should we settle at, finally?"

"Fifty less, that is all I can do."

"Then I don't want them. You keep them," Raghu said defiantly and began walking away. Saranya stood there disappointed, her eyes still fixed on the wings.

"Palani, put the wings away," the owner could be heard loudly instructing the assistant.

By the time they reached the scooter, Saranya was in tears. Raghu seemed not to notice that.

"We will get one from another shop, Ma," he said.

"No, Appa, let us buy this one. It is very beautiful."

"It is very costly, and we will get a better pair in another shop." He headed towards the scooter. Saranya stood there quiet, her face fallen, lips quivering, and eyes all wet.

Left with no other option, Raghu said he would take the wings. Saranya was overjoyed to hold it in her hands again. All the way back home, riding pillion on the scooter, she felt as if she was flying.

At night, she attached the wings on her back and looked at herself in the mirror, admiring her reflection and smiling. The mother and daughter discussed the role of the angel and nothing else that evening. Saranya went to bed early.

Next morning, Renu woke Raghu up very early. She seemed agitated.

"Come and see our child," she said in a worried voice.

Raghu switched the light on and saw Saranya. She was asleep, but she was moaning in pain and her face showed signs of discomfort. There were rashes all over her face and body.

"She has measles." Renu was very concerned.

"Make some neem paste and apply it on her skin," Raghu suggested. He also called his mother who lived in the village for advice. Renu called her mother on the other phone.

"Apply neem paste"; "keep her at home"; "give her cooling foods and drinks like tender coconut water", and many other instructions were given.

Raghu did not go to work that day. Saranya kept looking at the wings that were lying near her.

"So I can't go to school, Appa?"

"No, dear, you can't until the rashes subside."

"Can I never be an angel, Appa?"

"You will surely act in the play next year."

"We will buy the wings, Appa."

"Okay..."

"No...You will give it back to the shop, won't you?"

"I won't. Let the wings stay."

Saranya lay on the mat, looking at the wings resting against the wall.

For Saranya's sake, Raghu called the shop and bought the wings. Yet on the evening of the Annual Day celebrations, Saranya cried and cried. Renu could not console her.

After a week, the rashes disappeared. Saranya had lost some weight, and her lips looked pale.

Later one day, Renu called Saranya and said that if she put on the wings that she liked so much, they could take a picture.

"I don't want these wings. I will never take part in any function ever again."

"Why, sweetie? Are you angry?" Raghu asked.

"No, Appa. I am not an angel. I am just a school girl. I don't need these wings and all," she said, speaking like a grown-up.

What had happened? Why had she changed? It was impossible to understand. She put the wings away in the room where they stored old things. She no longer had the playfulness of a little girl in her. She busied herself with her studies and homework. Smiles became a rarity. She remained pensive even when her parents took her to the beach.

"What happened to you, my dear?" Raghu asked one day. He could not bear to see this change in his little daughter.

"I am not a child anymore," she snapped angrily.

Raghu's heart broke when he heard that.

It grieved him to think that she would never be the old Saranya again.

No Ordinary Thief

In 1960, the traffic was not as busy as it is now and this city was not as crowded. It was not called Chennai then, it was Madras. Like numerous others, Thekkan came to Madras seeking a livelihood. He was twenty-eight then. He did not know a single soul in Madras. Thekkan laughed to himself when he thought of that.

"Why would a thief need acquaintances?" he asked himself.

Yes, Thekkan came to Madras only to steal. Before that he had robbed people at temple festivals and in other crowded places like Palani, Tirupparankundram, Samayapuram and so on. Sometimes he snatched the gold jewelery worn by little girls on their ears or around their necks. Sometimes he took handbags, *hundi*s, purses or watches. He had, however, never robbed a house. Nor did he need to.

One theft a day was his motto. And if a day went by without a successful loot, he punished himself by starving. With the money he got from selling the stolen goods, he fed the street dogs. And perhaps because of that the dogs never barked at him.

It was hunger that made him steal for the first time. He was twelve then. His grandmother had gone to work at the dyeing factory, locking him out of the house. He was very hungry, and it was unbearable. Playing truant, he had been roaming here and there, looking for something to eat. When he could not find any food, he even considered eating leaves like goats and cows.

It was then that he remembered the tea stall next to Tilakar grounds. There was only an old man there to manage the stall, so it would not be difficult to steal one *vadai* from the plate on the sly. This was Thekkan's plan when he went there. As he had expected, there was no one at the stall except the old man. He asked Thekkan to watch over his stall for a bit as he wanted to go pee. Luck was in Thekkan's favour. He nodded, smiling. The moment the old man was out of sight, he ate vadais from the plate to his heart's content. Then he took the plate with the remaining vadais and left the stall, just like that. He gave free vadais to the boys he came across on the way.

Of the remaining vadais, he gave one to a little goat. Then he strung four or five vadais on a string and wore it as a garland round his neck. Even then there were some vadais left over. He stuck a vadai each on a cycle bell, a post box, and the closed door of a shop. Then he flung the empty plate into a well. Thekkan felt very happy that day. When he went to that tea stall again after a few days, the old man did not seem to recognise him at all. The desire to steal took root in his heart that very day.

He began with petty thefts. No person can steal without anyone knowing. Maybe the theft is not known at the time of the act, but it never remains hidden. And there are some who are capable of smelling theft. They can simply smell it, it is like a sixth sense. That is how Ebenezer became his accomplice. Ebenezer had never stolen anything, but he knew all the thieves. His only job was to sell stolen articles. On the day he first met Thekkan, he said, "You have the theft-line running across your palm."

"No, I don't," Thekkan denied.

"Show me your hand. I will tell you." Then Ebenezer himself turned Thekkan's hand and pointed to a line on his palm.

"See, this. I don't have that line. This exists only on the palms of thieves. That is the identifying mark."

"How do you know?" Thekkan asked.

"I have seen many thieves. You are a thief too."

Thekkan finally admitted that he was.

"A thief must not stay in the same place for long. He must constantly shift places."

"I know that."

"Then let us both go to Madurai. You steal and I will sell."

That is how they travelled to Madurai together. Thekkan did not steal at night because for some reason he felt that night was not the right time for stealing. He liked to steal during the day and that too in crowded places. But Ebenezer tempted him by saying that he could steal more if he went out at night. He identified a house behind the Tirupparankundram hill. It was a lonely house. They surveyed the residents of that house for several days.

It was a family of traders consisting of six persons. Two of them were men—one aged, the other probably his son or son-in-law. Every full moon night the two men went to some temple leaving only the womenfolk behind at home. That day would be the right day for stealing.

Thekkan was delighted to venture on his task in the bright light of the full moon. But there was one thing that scared him. There were two Rajapalayam dogs in that house who could sense a stranger from afar and leap at him. Thekkan wondered how he could deal with them. So he wrapped a piece of meat in a cloth. He planned to throw the meat at the dogs and divert their attention.

The house glowed like an open lotus blossom in the light of the moon. The people inside were fast asleep. In the bright moonlight the trees and plants looked mist-drenched and frozen. When he jumped over the rear wall, his eyes scoured the compound to see if the dogs were around. There was no sign of them anywhere, they seemed to be asleep too. He jumped in boldly. As soon as he took a few steps forward, the two dogs he had thought were asleep came running to pounce fiercely at him. But wonder of wonders! They did not bark at all. They just kept staring at him. He forgot that he had to fling the meat at them. Instead, he stretched his hands towards them.

They came to him like children running to their father. He stroked their heads. One dog licked his hand. He saw a yearning, a desperate plea in the dog's eyes. As he stroked its head, the dog's history unfolded before his eyes. With that one touch he knew everything about the dog's life from the time of its birth till that moment. It felt strange. Poor dog, it had been beaten and kicked a lot. They had singed his bum with something hot. When he felt the dog's pain, he said to it tenderly, "All your pain will vanish."

The dog nodded as though it understood what Thekkan said. Then he touched the other dog's head. Its past too unfolded before him at once. He blessed that dog too. The two hounds knelt before Thekkan in silence as though he alone was their master. He gently pulled their ears and stroked their body, calming them.

"There is no enmity between your kind and thieves. People create this ill-feeling between us."

The dogs sat very still, as though they were cast in stone. Thekkan entered the house, stole things with ease and came out.

He did not tell Ebenezer anything about this. Thekkan was utterly perplexed: how could he sense the dogs' history? But it certainly was an advantage, wasn't it? A blessing for a thief.

Thereon, no dog barked in the homes where he went to steal. He read through touch the sad histories of the dogs. Dogs live with men only because they are afraid of hunger, just like he was. But dogs do not know how to steal. They openly carry away the things they want to eat. And then they get beaten. They become man's slaves only because they are not cunning enough. So they kiss the feet of the one who feeds them.

You are not a slave to anyone. You are a dog. He made every dog that knelt at his feet understand this.

He grieved when he thought about the discrimination faced by dogs based on their colour and breed; when he thought about their illnesses, the loss of hearing, the loss of sight, and malformations such as shortened legs caused by careless breeding.

Through his touch, he healed the dogs, he cured their incurable pain. He was like the Redeemer of Dogs. He realised that what gave him more joy than stealing was the chance to help the dogs in those houses. Just for this reason, he went to rob different places.

A dog's story is written in words of pain and grief. From the time it is a pup, it can live only by raising its voice. A dog without a bark does not get to live; all voiceless dogs are killed. A dog is but its bark.

There are many kinds of dogs—lazy ones, fierce ones, loving ones, impatient and hasty ones, and cowards. The bitches care nothing for the males, while the wide-eyed pups are amazed by the world. A dog roams around scouting for food and becomes enraged when it is hungry. The strays on the streets loathe the kind that live as house pets. Fatigue sweeps over the dogs as they grow old, and their death is always painful.

Thekkan began to understand dogs through his burglaries. Once in drunken banter, Ebenezer asked him, "Why do dogs never bark at you?"

"That's what even I find strange."

"No. Your hand has a scent. A scent that only dogs can smell."

"What scent is it?"

"I don't know how to say it. Cooks have flavour in their hands, no? A doctor has a healing touch, right? Like that, this is a kind of power you have. It manifests itself as a scent. The dogs can sense it, and so they come to you and kneel down."

"I'm a thief. The dog's job is to catch me."

"But to the dogs, you are god. That is why they kneel before you like we kneel before god."

"I am not god. But when my hands touch a dog, I am able to see its past."

"Some people's hands are special. You are one of them. You may not be useful to men, but you can make dogs feel calm and peaceful."

"That is what is puzzling."

"You must not analyse miracles, Thekka. You will never get caught when you steal. Go and steal wherever you want to."

"What if I go to a house where there are no dogs?"

"Maybe the people who have a certain 'dogness' in them will kneel before you. That's what I think. You are no ordinary thief, Thekka."

Thekkan laughed at that.

"I am a street dog myself. Maybe that is why the dogs like me."

"Who decides by whom miracles may be performed? Jesus Christ himself was the son of a carpenter."

Thekkan was confused when he heard Ebenezer's words. But he assured himself it was a good thing that he had the power to heal dogs.

After coming to Madras, Thekkan realised that a city is the right place for stealing. The only problem was that there were too many thieves. There were over a hundred thieves for each street: some robbed as traders, some robbed as government servants, and some as policemen who stole with authority. Petty thefts too took place in plenty.

But the dogs in the city were in a worse condition than the human beings. Some pets were enclosed in rooms with no ventilation, kept tied with chains, and none of them got enough food. On the other hand, some lucky dogs paraded around in cars and ate only biscuits.

The best doctors attended on them. Then there were the street dogs in Madras who roamed around in groups. They had no idea what to eat and would even chew away at tattered clothes.

Thekkan stole with ease in Madras. One day, in a house he went to rob, he saw a mango tree that had withered. When he touched its branch, he could immediately see its past. The original residents of that house had nurtured it with love. They had hung a swing from its branch and swung on it. They ate under the tree, in its shade. The tree had flourished listening to the playful yells and screams of the children. Every season, it bountifully bore fruits. Squirrels and parrots came from far to eat its fruits. But one day the house became empty. The residents had lost their court case and an order was passed asking them to vacate the house.

An old couple then owned the house. For six months the house had remained locked. And then it was given on rent to a government servant. The new tenants just ignored the tree. They never stepped out of the rear door into the backyard. Slowly the tree lost its vigour and began to die. It stopped bearing fruits. The squirrels and parrots no longer visited.

Thekkan stroked the mango tree and said, "Memories are always disturbing. Erase them. Your happiness is in flowering, bearing fruits and ripening them. You can't go on grieving the separation from the ones who loved you."

The leaves nodded as though they understood.

"You must live," he encouraged the tree, holding on to the branches.

Ebenezer said that afterwards the tree revived. Its branches spread and became green once more and it began to bear fruits again. This happened not just with one mango tree. Abandoned guava trees, coconut trees, roadside neem trees—they all came alive and blossomed at Thekkan's touch.

Ebenezer told him again, "Thekka, your hands are miraculous. You are able to revive plants with your hands."

Thekkan disagreed.

"I am a thief. I am like a thorn shrub myself. Maybe that is why I am able to sense the lives of other plants just by touching them."

Thekkan did not stop stealing even after accomplishing these two miracles. He moved around different parts of Madras and kept thieving. Ebenezer lived in comfort selling the stolen jewels and silver.

One rainy season, Thekkan had gone to the Seven Wells area to steal. The place was desolate as it had just rained. One homeless family was looking for a place to sleep as the road where they usually stayed was waterlogged. They spread a piece of cloth on the steps in front of a closed shop. One little girl among them was weeping and refusing to sleep on the damp ground. The mother gave her a slap on the back.

"Sleep if you want, or stay awake," she snarled at the child.

The girl crossed the road and sat on the steps of a bank that was shut for the night. Thekkan kept staring at her. She was not afraid of him at all.

He went and sat next to her. He asked her if she was hungry.

She glowered at him.

"I want to sleep."

"Then sleep."

"There is no place."

"Will you be able to sleep if you put your head on my lap?"

She nodded. He helped her lie down as if she was his own daughter. She too lay down comfortably, clasping his hand in hers. As she held his hand, her future was revealed to Thekkan.

The girl is being dragged away by two policemen. In a place like an old car shed, they rape her. Blood flows down her thighs. She howls in pain. They beat her and break her teeth. She loses consciousness. They carry her and throw her in the garbage.

Then someone else finds her there and takes her away. They force her to beg. She begs in the train. She marries someone and has four or five children. Her children die young. She gets elephantiasis. Her husband deserts her. She goes around begging in the streets where dogs chase her. She weeps and wails. Her hair grows grey, her shoulder blades stick out. She lies under a tree unable to move her swollen, disfigured leg. A torn piece of cloth is spread out in front of her. Coins are scattered on it. She tries to reach out and collect the coins, but she is not able to. Feeling dizzy, she slips and falls and dies. There is no one to take her corpse away. Sanitary workers carry her away in their cart the next day. Crows hover above and keep cawing.

Thekkan was startled back to consciousness from his trance. The child was fast asleep.

His heart ached for the little girl. *Is this going to be her life? Can I do nothing to stop this, to change her future? Why did I have to know all this? If I told her that this is going to be her future, will she even believe me? Why was her future revealed to me?* He wanted to leave her there and go away. But since she was clutching his hand tightly, he could not get up. He stayed there till dawn.

His inability to do anything for that little girl filled him with sorrow. When in her sleep she happened to turn over, he slowly moved her head from his lap to the ground. Then he went to see Ebenezer.

Ebenezer said again, "You are not just a thief."

Thekkan was angry on hearing this.

"No, I wish to be just a thief. I don't want to know the past or the future. Let dogs bark at me. Let trees wither. Let anything happen to the girl. I just want to live."

Thekkan's tone frightened Ebenezer, but at the same time he also felt pity.

"I understand now why Jesus Christ accepted the cross."

Thekkan was unwell for a few days after that. He stayed at Ebenezer's house and did not go out at all. They finally decided to move to another town. So they took the train to Hyderabad. Even on the train, when Thekkan held a girl's hand, he could tell her future. That too was a sad vision.

Thekkan did not eat anything on the train. When they got down at Hyderabad station, the two of them decided to have tea at the tea stall there.

"I am going to cut my hand off. I cannot live with this," Thekkan said, biting into the butter biscuit while letting the tea cool off.

"Touch me and see if you can tell my future."

"No, I can see only the future of little girls. And I just cannot bear what I see."

"Thekka, a person who feels sympathy for another being cannot be a thief."

"There is only one way out. No other way."

"Then out with it."

"I want to be punished for my theft and sent to prison. I want to be sentenced for life."

"Don't be stupid. If you go to jail, what will I do?"

"More dangerous than the thief is the one who guides him. There is a shadow that always follows the thief, and that is the shadow of his guide."

"Thekka, do not look at me like that."

"I am going to kill you and go to jail. There is no other way. No other way to put an end to my 'miracles'."

Ebenezer went pale. He took out the pocket knife he hid in his pant pocket and tried to stab Thekkan.

In a swift move, Thekkan grabbed the hand that held the knife, twisted it and snatched the weapon away. He then stabbed Ebenezer in his abdomen. Ebenezer screamed as blood poured from his stomach. Those who were drinking tea at the stall shrieked in fear and ran away.

After stabbing Ebenezer near the tea stall at the crowded station, Thekkan slowly sipped on his tea. He could see the police at a distance, coming towards him. He wondered what story he should tell them.

A dog came and stood in front of Thekkan, its head raised. Thekkan stroked the dog's head and said—

"You are a street dog. So am I. We have nowhere to go. As long as hunger chases us, we have to keep running. But you will surely get food. All your miseries will end."

He spoke to the dog as though he was advising a child.

Then the police started to rain blows upon him. Three policemen beat him with *lathis* and dragged him away. The dog munching on the butter biscuit looked on.

In Search of Gandhi

I had arrived at Wardha just that morning. It was my first visit to the Gandhi Ashram there, though I had read a lot about it and also seen photographs. It looked just like any other run-of-the-mill old people's home. The ashram's deep significance was not apparent to the eye.

Rachel was taking pictures of the hut where Gandhi had stayed. It was a simple structure with a thatched roof. Gandhi's walking stick, footwear and writing materials were kept on display. Next to the bed stood a kerosene lamp.

"Was there electricity in this ashram during Gandhi's time?" Rachel asked me.

"I don't think so. But he would have surely realised that the spirit of the village would be changed by the advent of electricity."

How a man lives is determined by how he decides to address his needs. Gandhi seems to have been a person who had carefully thought about this.

It must have been a very moving experience for those who entered this room and saw him here. The scene flashed in my mind's eye suddenly—Gandhi would have been seated right there! He would not have sat still even for a moment. Impossible. He would have been busy doing something. Why was there such restlessness in his heart? I wondered why he thought rest was a sign of weakness.

Gandhi had lived treating every second of his life as precious. And here I am, completely different. I am defined by laziness, an all-encompassing dissatisfaction, and needless fear and anxiety. I had structured my life through education, while Gandhi had given up his education to embrace life with wide open arms and move forward. In the end, he lived like any other ordinary Indian farmer. In return, he received as his gift both the heights of hope and the depths of despair.

I truly believe we can never really understand Gandhi by just reading about him. What is registered through those readings is just our opinion of the image of Gandhi. We must live the pain, the austerity and directness underlying each of his actions. Only then will the essence of Gandhi fill us little by little, like grains of sand trickling down in an hourglass.

It was my mother who had introduced me to Gandhi when I was twelve. When I showed her the first prize I had won for my pencil drawing of Gandhi, she was very happy.

"Your drawing is very life-like. I have seen Gandhi, you know."

I did not believe her. How could my Amma have seen Gandhi? Maybe he had visited her village Pattaikulam. I asked her about it.

"No, he did not come to my village. I went in search of him and saw him at Wardha."

"Really? Are you telling me the truth?"

"It's a long story. You were not born then."

She then showed me her left hand, which was slightly bent and misshapen.

"This hand was broken because of Gandhi. You know who did it? Your Appa. This was the punishment he gave me for going to see Gandhi. Appa absolutely despised Gandhi. And not just your Appa, most men did not like him. It is natural, isn't it, for men who are power-hungry to dislike Gandhi? Women alone can understand him truly and deeply.

"When I went and stood before him in Wardha, I did not see him as a man, as a person who was different from me. I could not speak as my tongue had thickened into silence. I sobbed uncontrollably. Bapuji told me something, his eyes smiling with compassion. At that time, I did not know a single word of English or Hindi, so I did not understand his words. But I understood that he was comforting me.

"I had wished to remain in Wardha for the rest of my life. But I was not destined for such good fortune. All of a sudden, one day, your Appa came to drag me back. I refused to leave the ashram. But Bapuji gently stroked my head and told me to return. I have lived all these years with your Appa only because of Bapuji's words."

"Why did you go in search of Gandhi, Amma?"

Amma did not reply, she remained silent.

"You won't understand and I don't want to tell you." She shook her head and ended the conversation.

Thereafter, once or twice when that topic came up, I overheard my parents fighting.

"You slut! If it had been any other man, he would have cut you up and buried you!" Appa shouted in rage.

"Didn't you do that already, long ago?" Amma said calmly.

Appa glared at her and went out.

"Your father hates women discussing politics. He bitterly dislikes educated women...and then on top of that, she joined Gandhi's party! This is the reason for all the trouble between your parents." Venkataratnam Mama explained to me once.

At that age, I thought it was just marital problems, a matter between a husband and wife. But it was not that. I understood much later that it was the tension between love and hatred. When her conjugal life plunged Amma into darkness, it was Gandhi who had redeemed her. He had proved that it was possible to rise above all scorn and contempt if one was truthful in one's actions. He taught that the voice of conscience must be respected. Above all, he helped one understand that living for others may inflict pain, but it always brought greater peace in the end.

"Lats, actually Gandhi saved the world that god had abandoned. The same happened in your mother's life too. Two miscarriages, babies in quick succession, poverty, the indignity faced in a joint family structure...all these had smothered your mother, stifled her breath. At a time like that, it was Gandhi alone who was the lamp of hope in her life. More than Gandhi the social activist, it was Gandhi the simple hope who gave her the strength she needed. Those who understood this have always loved Gandhi."

Rachel was right. What Indian women saw in Gandhi was not the social reformer. When most people turned their backs on the basic values of dharma and adopted evil and falsehood, Gandhi, as a man of simplicity, had surrendered himself to the cause of righteousness and dharma. He had lived his life ceaselessly subjecting his actions to self-analysis.

Rachel knew violence. She was a Jew. She was first my student and then she married me. Now she was more attached to the women in my family than I was. She had once told me that it seemed like these women lived in permanent concentration camps. An undeniable truth.

"Latchuma, I want to visit London. Just once," Amma asked me on the phone one day. This was when I had decided to take up a job in London where I had gone to study economics.

Amma alone called me, Latchumanan, as Latchuma. The Londoners called me Lats. For Appa and my other friends, I was Manaa. But when Amma called me Latchuma, her voice soaked in a rare kind of love, it sounded like a girl's name.

"When I visit home next, I will bring you to London with me."

"No, *da.* I want to come all by myself, and that too by sea."

I understood why she wanted to come. It was her attachment to Gandhi that underlay her desire to see London. She wanted to experience how Gandhi felt when he went to London at nineteen years of age without knowing the language of the country. *What is this craze for Gandhi?*

"There are no ships making such trips now, Ma. If you want, you can come alone by flight," I said.

As she wished, Amma came to London all by herself. Her ripe old age had lent her a new radiance. She emerged slowly through the glass doors, dressed beautifully in a pink saree with an orange shawl wrapped around her, her hair as white as a stork's wings, and her face so pale it looked almost anaemic.

There was not a jot of fear in her eyes. She did not look at any of the passengers who walked past her. The image of her walking calmly and slowly towards the exit gate is still etched in my heart.

"Did they ask you anything at immigration?" I asked Amma, my voice strained.

"They asked me why I have come. I said just like that, *summa*, without any reason. The immigration officer laughed and said that those who come here just like that never want to leave London. He said 'You too will become like that, you will see.' I replied that my memories will not let me stay in a foreign land. He raised his eyebrows in surprise and said that my words were absolutely true. That was all." She looked out of the car window at the streets of London with excitement as we drove by.

In the last ten years, after Appa's death, Amma has spent all her time reading books, both in English and Tamil. When she read, it looked like she was studying for some exam. Sometimes with the book open on her lap, she sat in the chair talking to herself. Amma lived in a world of her own, an invisible world woven by herself, for herself.

Amma stayed with me in London for two and a half months. She took the tube and went around the city by herself to see all the places with a Gandhi connection—the University College, the streets through which Gandhi had walked, the Vegetarian Society of which he was a member. She did not talk to me much about all this. She occasionally spoke to Rachel about Gandhi.

It was very amusing to see Rachel and Amma in conversation. Amma treated her like a schoolgirl.

"Generally Indian women shake their heads a lot when they speak. But your mother does not. Why is that?"

It was only then that I even noticed this about my mother.

"You women observe minutely and notice everything. I don't know what to say." Quite puzzled, I laughed.

"I sometimes feel afraid when I talk to your mother. Buried deep in her eyes are many things that are unspoken. She is an unusual bird."

I liked it when Rachel called Amma an unusual bird. I too had felt she was like a bird. Not just any bird, but one in search of Gandhi.

I wanted to see what she was searching for through Gandhi, so I told her I would accompany her one day. She did not stop me. We took the train, had coffee at a café on Dover Street and went to an old library that Amma had been visiting.

Amma picked up a book which she had half-read and resumed reading it. Through the window near Amma's chair, I could see the city of London glowing. Amma had not chosen that spot just to sit and read. She was also internalising the energy and spirit of the city little by little.

She was absorbing within herself London's characteristic yellow glow and the dampness of its air. After a long silence, she spoke.

"When Gandhi came to London, he must have intensely missed his mother, being away from her for so long. This city intensifies the pangs of separation."

True. I have felt it too. All of a sudden, during my class at the University, something small would invoke the past and the dam inside would break, flooding my mind with the memories of lost relationships. The low mood would persist for a few days and then slowly drain away.

"Indians think a lot about the past regretfully. This is their strength as well as their weakness," Rachel observed.

She was right, but the regret is not just plain regret. It is a deeply personal emotion, a state that cannot be shared. When I am in a mood like that, I withdraw within myself and do not talk to Rachel.

She knew that. She understood me. Jewish women like Rachel prefer men's silences to their speech.

"Gandhi did not have very many memories of his father and found himself to have completely disengaged from him. His father was not a good father either. I see Gandhi and Buddha as men who sensed the feminine in themselves. There are many similarities between these two great men. In Gandhi you can find a reflection of the innermost depths, the essence, the *agam* of Indian women. It is strong and not easily quelled. Isn't the Gandhian weapon of fasting itself a women's symbol of resistance?" Amma said to me when we were in the library.

Amma had thought deeply about this. Books had taught her a lot. What was mere information for me had become a lived experience for her, that much I understood.

Apart from this, Gandhi did not fascinate me at all.

One day Amma and I walked all the way to Victoria Park. It was on this walk that Amma told me the full story of her escape to Wardha.

Amma was nineteen when it happened.

She was married off at fourteen. After her marriage, she remained at her mother's house for six months. Appa was then working as the Salt Inspector at Marakkanam.

It was the height of summer when Appa took her to the quarters allotted to him near the seashore to start their life together. There was no other human habitation near that house. The shining salt pans, the smell of salt heating up and melting, the frightening screeches of the cormorants, the sizzling heat—all of it combined adversely affected Amma's health. Fever and cough afflicted her frequently and she would stay up coughing all night. Unable to bear this, Appa took her to his aunt's house at Kollam and left her there.

It was there that Amma saw the freedom struggle marches for the first time. She and another girl called Narayani held flags in their hands and cheered the Congress members who were in the procession. One day the two of them went to the Bhangavathi temple and prayed for Congress' win. Soon after that, Amma began to hear about Gandhi from Neelammai, a servant who worked at their house.

"Susila, do you know what this man says? He says that men should not drink *kallu.* This alone is enough to prove his goodness. He has been beaten by the police and sent to jail. He washes his own clothes. Thaliyath Muthalali said that he even cleans the latrine himself. Isn't one who does all this the real leader?" Neelammai spoke about Gandhi with great wonder and respect.

Two days after she heard about Gandhi from Neelammai, Amma secretly went to the Congress meeting that was being held nearby. She heard a song about Gandhi at this meeting for the first time. It moved her deeply as she created an image of Gandhi in her mind.

Gandhi is a redeemer. He is engaged in the struggle for redemption and freedom of Indians from white men. A simple person, an incessant fighter.

Many speakers praised Gandhi at the meeting. As she listened to them, she was filled with the desire to see Gandhi.

While she was in Kollam, Amma conceived her first child. At once they sent her to her parents' place for a few months. There she got a book about Gandhi from Seenuvasa Mama and started reading it. As she read on, Gandhi took root in her heart and started to grow. There were so many questions she had about Gandhi, but she did not know whom to ask.

Appa then took her back to Marakkanam. The change of place and Appa's insatiable lust exhausted her. Her head constantly hurt because of the ceaseless roar of the sea and the torrid heat. The days stretched, empty and meaningless. Then she had a miscarriage. Because of the excessive bleeding, she became very weak. Appa sent a telegram to his father-in-law saying that he was saddled with a good-for-nothing and he must take his daughter back with him.

For a year and a half, Amma lived in her parents' place almost like a *vazhavetti*, a deserted woman. Gandhi was what saved her from falling into depression during that time. She spent her time spinning *khadi* on the *charkha* and listening to news about Gandhi. Then Appa came from Marakkanam one day. He spoke in a conciliatory way and took her back with him. Before they reached Madurai railway station, Appa picked a quarrel with Amma and right in the middle of the road, he hit her and broke her bangles. He left her there all alone on the road and left for Marakkanam by himself.

Appa's iron fist and his uncontrolled rage began to impact Amma's mental health, and she began shrinking into herself. She started shivering with fear at the mere mention of Appa's name. At this tumultuous time in her life, Seenu Mama started accompanying her to the library and helped her borrow books. That was the first step to Amma's transformation. The visits to Ratnam Chettiar Library gave her the solace she needed.

The desire to see Gandhi in person began to stir in Amma's heart, and around the same time, Appa was transferred to Thoothukudi. The loneliness and change of location had brought about some changes in Appa. He took Amma with him again. Soon, Amma become pregnant once more. This time it was a girl child that was still-born. Appa did not even look at the infant. He told them to bury it. Amma kept crying, grieving for the lost child. Appa never came near her except to have sex.

When she became pregnant again, he bought her a gramophone box. Amma did not like music as much as she loved books. She only wanted to read, but Appa did not permit her at all. The only printed text in the house was the piece of newspaper that the groceries—usually lentils and spices—came wrapped in. There was not a scrap of any other paper to be found in the house. Appa did not allow her to go to the local library either. It was then that my elder brother was born. When he was an infant, Amma's neighbour Jebamary became her friend. Jebamary brought books for Amma and Amma could only read them at Jebamary's house. One day, Jebamary said that her brother who lived in Nagpur could take Amma to see Gandhi and that there would be no difficulty.

At some point, Appa went to Vedaranyam to work on-site, and it must have been then that the idea to go to Wardha sprouted in Amma. The day after Appa's departure, Amma left the baby with Jebamary and set off. She told them that she was going to the temple.

She did not remember how she caught a bus to go to Madurai, or how she took the train to Chennai and then to Nagpur, and how she reached Jebamary's brother David's house. Some unknown force, some uncontrollable urge had transported her there.

Even when David had asked her to spend the night at his place, she had stubbornly insisted that she would not rest without seeing Gandhi. So that night itself they left for Wardha.

It was completely silent there when they reached because everyone at the ashram went to bed by nine. Amma was taken by surprise to find out that Wardha was a rural place with simple huts. *Is this where Gandhi lives? Is Wardha really such an out-of-the-way place?* They met Shyamlal, an ashram resident. He said that they could meet Bapuji in the morning during prayers.

That was the first time Amma heard Gandhi being referred to as Bapuji. She could not sleep that night. *Gandhi is sleeping in one of these huts nearby*. She wanted to rush to him as soon as it dawned and offer her respects.

The ashram residents got up as early as 4.30 a.m. Prayers commenced at 4.45. Amma took a bath in cold water and sat shivering, waiting to see Gandhi.

There were more than a hundred people in the ashram. One of them was a white woman. Amma wondered how this woman could work alongside Gandhi. Besides Amma, two persons with leprosy were waiting to see Gandhi. No one looked at them with disgust, they were showered with love instead. Treatment had not yet commenced for the day at Parchure Kuti where Manoharji Diwan treated patients free of cost.

There was a small hut called Mahadev Kuti right next to the hut in which Gandhi lived. Mahadev Desai stayed there. He was Gandhi's assistant and was deeply devoted to him.

In the early hours of the morning, when the sun had not fully risen, Gandhi had come to pray. There was no trace of sleep on his face which was ageing yet beautiful, with an unchanging smile, a child-like liveliness. He was accompanied by Rahim, a resident of Sevagram. As Gandhi walked along enquiring about the welfare of the residents, David introduced Amma to Gandhi.

"She has left her home and come away to see you."

"Are you married?" Gandhi asked, surprised.

Amma did not reply.

"She is married and has a child too. But she wanted to see you," David answered.

"What is there to see in me? I am a mere servant, a worker." With these words, he drew Amma close and touched her head comfortingly.

That touch broke the dam of her pain and tears flowed out. Gandhi possibly sensed the emotions behind her flooding tears.

"Thousands of Indian women like you are weeping in untold pain, Amma. Only god can give you comfort. I have only one thing to tell you: mental resilience and a fighting spirit are things I have learnt from women. You are like my own daughter. This house belongs to all. You can stay here for as long as you like. But you cannot live a life of ease. You must work—you must do social work, you must tend to patients. Can you do it?"

Amma did not understand a word that Gandhi spoke. But she consented to everything and nodded her head.

"Come now, my daughter. We will begin our work tomorrow with a prayer." Gandhi walked with Amma.

This is how Amma entered Wardha Ashram. Appa did not try to search for his wife. He was mad with rage. He called her names and left the baby with his sister and forgot all about Amma.

Amma stayed at Gandhi Ashram for two and a half months. The proximity to Gandhi educated her a great deal. Gandhi's gentleness got infused in her actions and speech, and one could see it in her eyes too. Amma worked as a nurse for the leprosy patients at the ashram. Mirabehn had taught Amma English. One day Amma and Mirabehn had gone to a church in Kolwada. Mirabehn played one of Beethoven's exquisite melodies on the piano there and Amma wept as she listened.

"Beethoven is the god of music, and Gandhi is the god of service," Mirabehn had said, holding Amma's hands in hers. In the two and a half months there, Amma had learnt to spin the charkha and got used to the ashram routine.

One must wake up at 4.30 a.m.; prayers at 4.45; classes for one hour from 5.15; work in the kitchen from 6.30 to 7.30; breakfast before 8, then gardening; medical service till lunch at 12.00, after which each one washed her own plate, and then rest. At 2.30 spinning yarn on the charkha, then classes again, followed by a joint discussion or on some days, there could be lectures. The evening meal must be over by 5.30. Night prayers began after sunset. Then everyone chatted amongst themselves, and sometimes there would be music. By 9 p.m. they went to sleep.

This simplicity and discipline of the ashram had transformed Amma entirely. Amma had completely forgotten the past she had left behind. Once, Mahadev Desai asked Amma to take his letter to Gandhi. When she entered his room, she saw that Gandhi had placed some shells as paperweights on his table.

"Bapuji, these shells are beautiful."

"They are from the beach at Porbandar. I have kept these shells with me since my childhood. I even took them with me to London. They are my constant companions. They share in silence with me the memories of my home. Every person keeps with him a thing that reminds him of the past. Others may not understand its significance." Bapuji laughed.

Sometime later, Appa came to Wardha with Seenuvasa Mama. Amma refused to go with them, but they insisted she should return home. Amma went to get Bapuji's blessings.

Gandhi spoke to her calmly, "I am unable to stop the violence that exists within the family structure. In this, I really see myself as a defeated man. I realise that no big transformation can be effected in India without the full partnership and support of women. I am now advising you as a mother would her daughter. It is a challenge to live in a space that crushes you. But it must be faced. This servant has no word of advice to give to a woman with a heart as pure as yours. But I promise to stay firm on my course of action because of the trust people like you have reposed in me. Since you are one of those who has infused that confidence in me, I owe you my gratitude."

Amma wept and wept. She wept more loudly than she had when she first saw Bapuji. Bapuji stood calmly looking at her. Appa dragged Amma to the train at night without uttering a single word. After they reached home, he broke her arm for having gone in search of Gandhi. That is how he punished her.

After narrating the entire story, Amma said, "Latchuma, do not think this is a rare incident, something that happened only with me. There are hundreds of women who have suffered the same. They have never forgotten Gandhi. Gandhi is always shining within them."

Until we reached home, the thought of Appa's terrible treatment of Amma is what kept gnawing at me even more than Amma's running away to see Gandhi. I wondered if I should apologise to her on his behalf. I did not know how to erase the bitterness she felt towards a dead man.

That night Amma and Rachel were watching a Tamil movie together on TV and laughing. Oddly, I loved to see their intimacy.

"Do you like Gandhi?" I asked Rachel when we were in our bedroom.

"You Indians dislike Gandhi without reason, you have a Gandhi-hating syndrome. You often treat him like garbage, and that saddens me deeply."

"Why do you say that?"

"I have not read about Gandhi much. But I feel an affinity towards him when I see his photographs. Just look at his innocent smile. I can say with confidence that a person who smiled like that would surely have lived with high principles. Just one or two things that I have heard about him were enough to make me like him. The truth is that it is when we know too much about someone that we begin to dislike them. Gandhi, to me, is like a distant star. Its radiance attracts me, but I have no desire to go close and learn more."

I hugged Rachel tight.

It proved to me again that women have a different approach to Gandhi, a deeper understanding of him.

"Amma, I want to read Gandhi's autobiography. Please get it from the library sometime," I said.

"People who hurry to meet Gandhi hurry to escape from him too." Amma laughed and so did I.

Amma did not bring Gandhi's *My Experiments with Truth* from the library. Six months after she had returned to India, I told her one day over the phone—

"I want to see Wardha. I think you should come with us."

"I am reminded of the lines in that poem...'The wings that are shed from the bird will not stick to her again.'"

"Do you hesitate to visit the ashram now since Gandhi is longer there?"

"This broken arm reminds me of Gandhi every day. I don't need to go to Wardha to renew my memory."

I gave up the plan since I knew Amma could not be swayed from her resolve. But after she died, Rachel reminded me.

"Lats, let us go to Wardha once for your mother. We definitely need something to remind us of the past."

That is how Rachel and I landed in Wardha. Ever since we arrived she was busy taking pictures.

I found it hard to believe this was Wardha Ashram. Why have they maintained this ashram like it is a place for the destitute? I could not see anything around me pulsating with positive energy. I could not see any signs of fascination for Gandhi either among the residents or the visitors. As if it was just an ordinary refuge.

We stayed there till the evening. As we left, Rachel said to me with a deep sigh, "Indians are a truly strange people. They always act counter to what they like. The problem is that they are unable to understand Gandhi even today. I am struck with wonder by this mystery. Gandhi's acts and thoughts in fact question our weaknesses, our defects, and they awaken our conscience. But this angers people. Gandhi is a thing of amusement for today's youth, a football they can kick around. What puzzles them however is that no matter how much they kick, this ball always comes back to its natural state.

"Every young Indian wants to kill Gandhi. But it is not so easy. This defeat leaves them with a bitter taste. There is only one way to go past Gandhi, and that is to consecrate him. Make him a saint, a superman! And you have achieved this successfully. Gandhi today is a mere image, a mere statue. This generation has not heard his voice. By chance I heard it on the internet one day, but I could not listen to it fully as tears began to flow from my eyes. He is impossible to...How do I say it...I don't know—he is pure, he has touched our hearts.

"What he says is not so important, but in whatever he says there is compassion and selfless purity. That is why I like him. Sometimes he is like my father, sometimes he is like my unborn child. That is all I can say." She was quiet for a while after this.

With Rachel's help I began to create my own Gandhi thereon. I had been one of those who wanted to kick around the idea of Gandhi. I cannot actually say I hated Gandhi. But I had been one of the millions who without reason pushed Gandhi far away. To go near him, one must make an effort because many reasons to hate him have already been established for us.

Is there another man like him who has faced such horrible abuse, such vile insults and criticism? Yet the charisma of Gandhi remains ever brilliant. One might even say that to hate Gandhi is to prepare oneself to start loving him.

If a person delves deep within his inner self, he or she will certainly feel Gandhi's presence. That person can then no longer hate Gandhi. He would have to pardon himself for pretending to hate Gandhi. But the world needs Gandhi haters, and there were many such people even when he lived.

Gandhi is a wind of purity. It is impossible to predict when it will become fierce and when it will calm down. But either way all dust and impurities are blown away by its force.

Many thoughts kept circling in my mind on my journey back as I began to read the copy of *My Experiments with Truth* that I had bought. We returned to London in two weeks after visiting the Gandhi Museum in Madurai, Porbandar, Sabarmati and Delhi. Suddenly books on Gandhi began to fill my house. I started to discuss and argue about Gandhi with everyone.

"Lats, you have begun to worship Gandhi. That is not the way to experiment. Try to understand him and live like him. Like your mother did.

"Gandhi called his book *The Story of My Experiments with Truth*. The word 'experiment' is not a casual term: it means an activity, a scientific process. There was a scientist within Gandhi who constantly studied himself. Indians tend to mystify the body, but I think Gandhi was the first Indian who did not do that.

"Gandhi does not lean on the walking stick. He holds it to accompany him. The walking stick is for him a tool to accelerate his pace, Lats. Memories are stirred less by what is than what is not. It is the same in Gandhi's case too." Rachel smiled.

I thought I saw a trace of Amma's smile within Rachel's. I hugged her close to me.

Remember, You Are Thirty-Four Now

"Remember, you are thirty-four now," Appa told Suganthi as she was leaving for work.

Irritated, she turned and glared at him.

"So what?"

Appa gazed down at the paper as if he was reading it. It was one of his tricks, a way he teased her.

Because she was already late for office, she didn't want to fight with Appa. If it had been a holiday, this exchange of remarks would surely have ended in a big fight. Appa always started this just when she was leaving for work. In the beginning she thought that he said this just to hurt her, but as she heard it again and again it palled on her. It now sounded like one of those reminders—"The light is still on" or "The gas has not been turned off"...something like that.

She never felt she was thirty-four. She had felt the distinct passage of time only during her school years. When she entered college, she suddenly felt as if many years had gone by. Even after the four years in engineering college, she did not feel like she had grown older even though the years had gone by.

She first worked in Bengaluru and then got transferred to Mumbai. It was only later when she was in the USA for a year and a half that she felt the passing of the years.

Even then, the mirror did not betray her. But suddenly one day she felt herself ageing. To be precise, it was one day when she was hungry that she felt it. It was past 2.30 and she felt an urgency to go to the canteen to eat. She told herself that she would finish her work first and then leave. But she could not wait. *What is the big hurry? So what if I feel hungry?* she thought. But her body rebelled and her hands began shaking. That is when she realised she was thirty-two. Was she the only person who suddenly felt their age when hunger hit, or did it happen to everyone?

Suganthi did not discuss this with anyone. She usually had her food alone. Is eating alone the first sign of ageing? She thought it was. The canteen was crowded. She would eat whatever was available. She bought *thayir vadai* and sat down. She did not know when she ate it, but after a while her plate was empty.

When she returned to her seat at the desk, she was overcome with tiredness. Her feet went numb and she felt heavy like a statue made of stone. She stirred and loosened her limbs. She looked around and all the things surrounding her looked aged, including Keshav who stood there laughing. It was clearly evident that everyone had grown old.

Many try to hide their age, while some use it as a weapon and some use it to beg. That day when Suganthi returned home she felt as if she had turned sixty or seventy.

She threw herself on the bed and cried. She did not know why she was crying. But she cried for a long while. Then she got up, washed her face and decided to go out for dinner. She called an auto and went to Besant Nagar.

While in the auto, she looked at everyone on the road and tried to guess their age. She was almost at the door of the restaurant when she realised she did not want to eat. *Shall I walk to the beach and sit there for a while? Or shall I go to my home town and spend a week there?*

She used to visit her family once in six months. Her father had retired and lived in her elder brother's house. The moment she reached his house, her brother would start a sermon. He would advise her as though she was still a school girl. Appa did not advise her much, but he would keep staring at her as if she had done something wrong. The silence was worse than the speech. When they sat down for meals, her sister-in-law would sometimes say something deliberately hurtful. And sometimes in response, Suganthi would blurt out a retort as acrid as their comments. Once it made her sister-in-law return to the kitchen crying. She was about two years younger than Suganthi. Did she consider herself more qualified merely because she was married and had children? After that she never visited her elder brother again. Her younger brother was in London. He was also married and his in-laws lived in Tiruvanmiyur. So he had bought a new house near his in-laws'. Not once had he invited her to visit him. One occasional phone call was all that comprised their relationship. Do people grow apart as they grow older?

Suganthi was well aware that she was growing old. She felt age creeping up to her every time she planned a visit to her home town. Every place has its own norms, its own ideas of what age is old. In cities, until you are forty you are young, but in villages being forty is standing at the threshold of old age. Then they start calling you *perusu*, an oldie.

When it comes to age, men and women are not seen through the same lens. For men, it is only at forty that their sexual urges and desires start peaking, but for women at forty, their desires are fast draining—all they want is to have autonomy and to travel without a mate.

Age creeps up noiselessly like a snake and slithers past us. When she was five, the mirror on the cupboard was out of her reach, and so she had wanted from the bottom of her heart to grow older and taller in a single day. But does age pay heed to anyone's wishes? No.

During her school days, she had stood for hours before the mirror, adjusting her half-saree, smoothing down her eyebrows, and twirling the locks near her ears. Age then was a perfumed oil that lent more fragrance the more you rubbed it in. She appeared beautiful to herself in whatever dress she wore. She often smiled to herself in the mirror. She alone knew the reason behind that smile.

But in her college days she did not give much thought to her age. It accompanied her like a shadow, gradually growing, but she paid no attention to it.

It was Appa who counted her passing years more keenly than she did. It was not just her father though, every father starts dreaming of his daughter's wedding as soon as she is born. The anxiety of finding her a good husband fills them drop by drop. For the mother, the wedding is not an issue; her worry is about her daughter's life after her marriage. Amma would constantly harp on that. Amma believed that someone would surely get married to Suganthi. But Appa did not think of this lightly. He had visualised an image of a son-in-law who was to his liking and to Suganthi's liking, a man who was well-off, educated and good overall. Though he knew that he would not find a man with all of these qualities, he could not give up hope. During her first year in college, Suganthi had many dreams of her marriage—she even thought she could possibly pursue her studies after marriage. But such dreams had disappeared when she was in her final year.

Once she started to work, she asked herself: *Why should I get married?* By the time she returned from the USA, she had made up her mind not to marry and decided instead to live alone.

Appa did not understand her decision at all. He fought with her sometimes, and he had even wept on occasion. But Suganthi was never affected by her father's tears. She believed that for men, shedding tears too was a ruse. For months, Appa would stop talking to her. To her, it was no loss. Then one day when she was back from office, he told her that he would never again broach the subject of marriage.

Suganthi never tried to find out why.

She took Appa to Adyar, where he had his eyes tested and then she bought him new spectacles.

"Your hair has greyed a lot. Put on some hair dye," Appa told her that night at dinner, wearing the new spectacles.

"Why should I?"

"Otherwise, the grey hair shows."

"Let it show. It does not matter."

"It is for your good, Ma."

"I know what is good for me, Appa."

"Will you never listen to what Appa says?"

"When have you ever said something that is worth listening to?"

"The only mistake I ever made was educating you."

"That is the only reason I can still respect you."

"You are already thirty-three."

"So what?"

"Shouldn't you have a life of your own?"

"What do you mean 'life of my own'?"

"Marriage, Ma."

"It did not seem that Amma led a very full life by marrying you."

"She died early..."

"Appa, this is my life. This is enough. I will remain like this."

"You can't remain like this, Ma."

"Why not?"

"I have seen many people whose lives were ruined."

"You want mine to be ruined too?"

"It's not that, Ma. Age, once gone, will not come back."

"I don't care."

"Tell me, who will marry you when you are fifty?"

"Why should I marry? I will say 'enough' to life and just die."

"Now you are just arguing for the sake of it."

"Is there nothing to discuss except marriage, husband and children? Leave it, Pa."

"If I touch this topic again, hit me with your slippers."

Appa went and locked himself in the toilet. *It is stupid if you think that sitting there stubbornly for hours, sulking, would help people understand you*, Suganthi thought.

When she did not pay heed to his direct advice, he began to ask relatives and colleagues to talk to her about this.

Suganthi was totally fed up. It was she who had asked Appa to come and stay with her. The reason was that she faced unbearable problems as a woman living alone in an apartment. Earlier, she was staying in a ladies' hostel. It was like a prison, full of restrictions. Worse than that were her roommates, who were jealous and resentful, and behaved very badly. She could not get along with any of the other hostel residents either. Thrice her salary was stolen. Bad-mouthing others, gossiping and stealing were routine activities. One of her roommates referred to her, well within her earshot, as someone past the "expiry date". Suganthi just could not bear this remark and hurled choice insults back at her. The girl went and complained to the warden, who in turn made fun of Suganthi, saying it was expected that "stale objects" would be like that. She then asked Suganthi to vacate.

After this, Suganthi rented a flat and moved in. In a few days she realised that men were under the impression that they could freely knock on the door of a woman who lived alone. Men of all ages misbehaved with her. After a while, she had asked her father to come and stay with her.

A few days later, her father asked her, "Are you in love with anyone?"

She had been expecting her father to ask her this for many years. When he finally did, she glared at him.

"No."

"It doesn't matter who it is, I will talk to him and arrange everything."

"Why? Don't I know how to do it myself?"

"Then why do you say that you don't want to get married?"

"I never said so."

"Then why don't you?"

"I have never felt like it."

"Then that means you don't want to, isn't it?"

"You can think that if you want."

"If you had got married at the right time, your daughter would have been in school now. But I don't have the good fortune to witness that, do I?"

"Both your sons are married and their children are going to school. Enjoy that to your heart's content. Isn't that enough?"

"Fine, roam around like a lonesome monkey. Who can ask you anything?" Appa was furious.

That day Suganthi broke down. Her father did not expect that. He tried consoling her and said, "Would you want to go to a psychiatrist for some counselling?"

"Why, Appa? To check if I am mentally sick?"

"Not that. But this has to do with the mind too, that's why I suggested."

"But you always say that I am thirty-four, I am outdated. That is why I am crying."

He did not respond. He had the newspaper open, he went back to reading it. That night neither of them ate anything. When she woke up next morning, he was not there. He had left a note saying that he was going back. She tore it up. She realised that there was no one for her in this world and went to work.

One day, when returning home, in the bus, she was suddenly reminded of Avvaiyar. They say Avvaiyar became an old woman overnight. Why did she become an old woman? She could have become an eight-year-old girl...then she could have enjoyed a few more years.

One night some weeks later she invented a fantasy. She began to imagine that with her there lived a man she loved, two children, and a pet parrot. She started talking to them. She told stories to her imaginary children. She started believing that there were people in the house with her all the time. At first it was like a game. Then slowly she began believing it as the truth.

As if to prove the existence of her imaginary family, she washed a T-shirt, a pair of jeans and kids' clothes and hung them on the clothes line. These invisible persons gave her much comfort.

Isn't this what life is? It is our imagination that makes our lives liveable, happy. The truth may not be happy.

After this she started coming home from work as early as she could. She began to feel that hereafter she would not grow any older.

Even while at work, she would think of the imaginary persons at home and smile to herself. Then one day she began wearing *metti* like a married woman. Her colleagues wondered about the change that they spotted. But no one asked her anything.

One early morning, the doorbell rang. It was her father. She asked him to come in. He saw the clothes drying on the line and asked whose clothes they were.

She did not reply.

Following her father's arrival, she started believing that all those people who had been staying with her had gone out of town. Her heart ached because of the emptiness she felt. She hid the pain and attended to her work. Appa saw the metti on her toes and asked her why she was wearing them.

"Because I like them."

"Have you married some guy secretly?"

She shook her head to say no.

"Then have you gone mad?" Appa started ranting again.

She ignored him and was stepping out to go to office. At that moment, her father said, "You are thirty-four. Remember that. You may not listen to me, but know that your body will also not listen to you as the years pass by. At least get that into your head."

Anger bubbled up within Suganthi. But she controlled herself because she was getting late for office. As she was going down the lift, a thought struck her.

Instead of our age growing in the ascending order, it can decrease and go backward, can't it?

Let age go in whatever direction for the rest of the world, but she must start believing that for her it goes backwards. She thought that today she would lie to her colleagues, tell them that it was her thirty-third birthday. She would cut a cake and share it with them.

The moment she thought that, she felt that her age was rapidly decreasing and that she had become a school girl once more. As she sat in the bus, she kept thinking of the cake that she had to buy. Everything around her appeared new—the roads, the people, the vehicles, the trees, the sky, the birds...everything. She smiled to herself.

And then suddenly it hit her, the absurdity of it all. She could not control herself and began to cry. She did not mind that she was crying in front of everyone in the bus.

Should she hide everything just because she was growing older?